keep giving me love

BRIANN DANAE

trigger/content warnings

Grief
Abandonment
Childhood Trauma
Loss of Parent
Alcoholism

To the ones who decided to let love in. It feels good to share it with someone else, doesn't it?

- BriAnn Danae

contents

one

JUNE 2023

Synovi used to pray for days like these.

Back when he still had hope that his life would one day change for the better, he imagined having no worries, no stress, no doubts about being wanted and then abandoned, and more than anything... having something to call his own.

SB's Cleaning Service was just that.

One good deed had changed his life forever. Saving Racquel outside of the club that night lived rent-free in his mind. Had he not been a real man and been raised right by his GiGi, life as he knew it today wouldn't have been the same. As much as things had gone wrong in his life, Synovi couldn't front like the one he lived now wasn't worth the hardships he'd endured.

Had he questioned why he had to go through so much to make it here? Absolutely, but he never gave up. His faith wavered, but he never stopped trusting in God to come through. On those days when he didn't know what to pray for, figuring his prayers didn't matter, he recited Galatians 6:9.

And let us not be weary in well doing: for in due season we shall reap, if we faint not.

It was easier said than done, but it'd been done. Remaining steadfast and being properly loved on placed Synovi in the position he was in today.

Reaping the benefits of his resilience and hard work, he sat behind his desk inside SB's office building, now coined SBCS, reviewing the weekly schedule for his employees.

Boss shit.

Entrepreneurial duties he enjoyed doing even though he now had an assistant for that. He wasn't above clerical work at all. Coming up on the one-year mark of officially being in business, Synovi was grateful to have an office building to operate out of. Three months into his contract with Bostyn, he quickly realized that navigating out of a storage unit wasn't going to cut it. Thankfully, Bostyn owned multiple properties, and Synovi viewed a few before setting up shop for SBCS. He could already see himself expanding in the future, but this would do for now.

Providing a space where his employees could stash their cleaning supplies, re-up on products, report updates, and check in with him was beneficial in more ways than one. With a staff of fifteen, keeping track of their everyday assignments was much easier handled from one location.

"We need to move someone over to Thursdays with Aja. That property is too big for one person."

Sitting in front of his desk, Eboni, Synovi's assistant, scrolled through the scheduling app on her iPad.

"Which property is that?" Synovi questioned.

"The five-bedroom house in Gladstone."

Synovi nodded. "She wasn't supposed to be out that way, to begin with," he grumbled. "Anybody else available?"

Eboni scrolled and made a few clicks. "Yep. Whitney is. She'll just be finishing up a job in North Kansas City, so she can meet her there afterward."

"Bet. You can adjust the schedule."

Eboni chuckled. "Oh, I was going to do that anyway."

Realizing he couldn't do everything on his own, Synovi posted a job listing online. The growth of SBCS was spoken into existence, but it still shocked Synovi by how swiftly it happened. He'd gone from residential to commercial cleaning in months and posted the job listing for an assistant with no high expectations.

Just shy of a year from having her son, Eboni was finally ready to return to work. Long before she'd gone on maternity leave from her administrative assistant job at a behavioral health center, she knew she wanted something different and much more flexible. As Synovi's assistant, she gained an increase in pay, was able to work from home when she wanted, and received a discount on services. It'd been four months since she took the position, and Eboni didn't see herself leaving anytime soon.

A notification popped up on Synovi's screen with the

shift update. Aja, Whitney, and all other employees would receive the update in the scheduling app.

"Don't forget you have a meeting with Mike from Dendrite Homes & Construction on Friday," Eboni reminded him.

"Yeah. Ten o'clock, right?" Synovi asked.

"Mhm. If that man buys one more property," she fake fussed.

Synovi smirked. "Let him. That's putting more money in our pockets."

"True," Eboni surmised just as her phone rang. "You mind if I take this? It's my husband."

"Nah. Handle yo' business."

One thing about working for Synovi, he was flexible and willing to work with you as long as you worked with him and did your job. He didn't have any kids, but some of his employees did, and he made sure to accommodate them as best as he could. Being understanding and having empathy came with being an employer. What didn't come with the role was letting people who were only looking for a quick buck tarnish his name and reputation.

Synovi gritted his teeth as Eboni headed out of the office, almost running into Tae, one of his employees.

"What's up, Eb?" Tae grinned, waltzing into the office like everything was good.

At least he's on time, Synovi thought. A sense of pride washed over him, spotting the SBCS navy blue work shirt Tae was wearing. Some days, it was still hard to fathom that he owned a successful business named after himself.

"You sure grinning hard for someone who might be out of a job," Synovi said.

The grin on Tae's face was replaced with a scowl. "What you mean, cuz? I ain't do shit to get fired."

Synovi's head tilted to the right. "Yeah? So, if I pull up this video footage from the Wright's house you cleaned the other day, everything gon' pan out?"

Smirking, Tae sat in the chair next to Eboni while tugging on one of the sprouting curls in his low-cut afro.

"I mean, shit. It might."

"Quit bullshitting with me. I ain't in the mood," Synovi expressed sternly. "I gave you an opportunity to put some money in your pocket and stay out the streets, and you stealing from my customers? Folks who keep the business going around here? That's what type of shit you on?"

"Man, them rich mothafuckas didn't need it anyway," Tae pressed.

"Not being able to be trusted is a character flaw. I ain't take you for that type of person, but I guess I was wrong." Synovi shrugged.

When Tae showed up for his interview with a résumé with hardly any work experience listed, Synovi didn't hold that against him. He knew what it was like growing up in the hood and not being given a chance. He also knew what it was like to get to the bag by any means necessary without taking from someone else's plate. Having people with integrity on his team was the only type of people Synovi wanted.

"I'm not that type of person," Tae defended himself. "Shit was just tempting. I can put it back."

Synovi gave him an icy glare. “That’s not the point. It’s the principle. Just ’cause something is tempting doesn’t mean you fall for it. That’s some gullible, weak nigga shit. That lets me know, for the right price, you’d do anything ’cause it sounds good.”

He tried to keep it professional, but his temper was about to get the best of him.

Tae sucked his teeth. “Now, you trying to hoe me.”

“Nah, I’m trying to teach your young ass some responsibility and accountability before you end up behind bars for some petty crime. Them folks could’ve easily gone to the police with proof and had you locked up. Instead, they came to me, and now you sitting up here, trying to act like I’m crazy.” Synovi chuckled, but there wasn’t a damn thing comical about playing with his business.

Sobering up after hearing that, Tae cleared his throat. “You right, cuz. It wasn’t even worth it. That was my first time even doing some shit like that.”

“That I know of,” Synovi added.

“That was the first time in general. It won’t happen again, though.”

Synovi shook his head. He didn’t know if Tae was remorseful or not, but he was about to find out.

“So, how you think we should handle this moving forward? I can’t trust you not to steal from folks' homes, so maybe this ain’t the job for you.”

“You ain’t gotta fire me, cuz. Just don’t have me clean their place again.”

Synovi’s laugh confused Tae.

"So, that's it, huh? Just move you to another crib with no disciplinary action?"

"Nah, I mean... do what you gotta do on that end, but I don't get no warning or nothing?" Tae wanted to know.

As badly as Synovi wanted to keep lecturing him, he didn't. He hoped life didn't show him that there was no warning when it came to it. While he could've easily fired him and taught him a lesson that'd stick with him, Synovi did him one better.

"I shouldn't give you anything, to be straight up. Me or this world don't owe you anything. There are consequences for the choices you make, and I know you know that. You fucking with my money and reputation, but I'ma give you a second chance 'cause there was a time in my life when I didn't receive one. I didn't let that stop me, though."

Synovi would never forget the day he was permanently removed from Solace Place. Considering his progress since living there, it was a bittersweet and humbling moment, but none of that mattered once he broke the rules. In his eyes, it was for the best. It only made him grind that much harder to never be in that position again.

"I hear you. I ain't trying to be labeled as no thief and tarnish yo' name and shit. It was no reason for me to be pocketing them folks' belongings," Tae said. "My impulsive side kicked in." He chuckled lowly.

"You got ADHD?" Synovi questioned seriously.

"Nah. Why you ask that?"

"Impulsivity is a symptom of ADHD. Control your urges, man. I ain't trying to preach to you, but you need to feel where I'm coming from 'cause I'm not giving any more chances after this one."

Tae nodded, and Synovi continued.

"If you ever see something another person got and you want it, work for that shit the same way they had to. The reward is much more satisfying when you know you put that work in and accomplished a goal. Taking from others won't get you far in life; if it does, it comes with sacrifices. One's money can't buy."

Fully understanding what he meant, Tae cleared his throat. He didn't have to be told the sacrifices Synovi mentioned. He'd witnessed plenty of people in his life jeopardize their livelihood for foolish acts. Reckless behaviors that should've been nipped in the bud. So, Tae was thankful for the guidance. At nineteen, he still had some maturing to do, and Synovi was sure to help him.

"Yeah, you right about that. Guess I needed the reminder. 'Preciate you for not firing me. So, what happens next?"

Synovi wasn't looking for an apology and was glad Tae didn't offer one. He was positive he wasn't sorry for his actions, only remorseful because he'd gotten caught.

"I'm putting you on disciplinary probation," Synovi stated.

Tae sucked his teeth. "Damn, a'ight. For how long, and what I gotta do?"

A few seconds passed, and Synovi said, "Two months. Nah, don't look like that. Two months is a cake-walk. You lucky I ain't say six."

Sixty days was better than being fired, so Tae kept his comments to himself.

"You can't call in or be late to work for any of those days. You can only clean office buildings, and you can't pick up any extra shifts."

Tae's eyes enlarged. "No extra shifts? Man, that's dead wrong. Them extra shifts be clutch as hell on a slow week."

Synovi wasn't trying to hear all that. "I could just fire you. Won't have no shifts at all."

"Nah, nah." Tae chuckled. "I'm good with that. When does my punishment start?"

"Today," Synovi answered before his personal phone rang. "Hol' up for a second," he told Tae while swiping his thumb across the screen of his iPhone to see what Racquel wanted.

Considering it was the middle of the day, it couldn't have been much, but he should've known better.

"What up, sis?" he answered.

"Um, hey. Are you busy? I know you probably are, but I need a favor."

Synovi smirked. "I'm at the office handling some business, but what you need?"

"Can you come pick me up, please?"

Her question was asked in a whining yet frustrated manner. Synovi was used to her tone, but the question presented made Synovi more alert.

"Yeah. Where you at?" He stood from his desk, not needing any further details besides her location. He'd get all of that when he got there.

"What's the name of these apartments, again?" he heard Racquel ask someone.

Synovi listened intently, picking up on the noisy background of chatter and rap music.

"Why? You ain't 'bout to have someone pull up over here," a dude Racquel had just met an hour prior said.

"Yes, I am since you said an Uber or Lyft won't come this way," Racquel sassed back with a roll of her neck.

Synovi's jaw ticked. "Aye. I'ont need the name. Share your location with me. I'm walking out now."

"Okay. I'm sharing it now," Racquel said.

"Bet. I'll see you in a minute. You safe?"

He couldn't help but ask. Taking in her surroundings, Racquel wouldn't consider the illegal activities around her safe, but she wasn't in danger. Just annoyed and ready to leave.

"Yes, I am." She sighed.

Synovi told her okay and hoped it remained that way. With a wave of his hand, Synovi motioned for Tae to come on.

"I'm sliding with you?" Tae asked in a hyped tone. He was with the shits and happy to be off work.

"Yeah. Don't get too excited. You still on the clock," Synovi told him as they walked down the hall. He stuck his head into Eboni's office. "Yo, Eb. I gotta handle some family business right quick. Can you have all my calls forwarded to you?"

"Yes. Is everything okay?" Eboni asked.

"It better be," was all Synovi said.

Racquel was always getting into some shit, which shouldn't have been anything new to Synovi. He hoped he didn't have to give out any more lectures for the day, but it looked like he'd be doing just that once he noticed Racquel's location.

"The fuck she doing in KGs?" Synovi grumbled.

He just knew those girls she considered her friends had her over there. Racquel was much too green to be posted up in the heart of the hood. At least, that was what Synovi thought.

"You said she where at?" Tae asked, closing the passenger door to the truck.

"Kennedy Gardens."

Tae grinned. He was born and raised in Kennedy Gardens, affectionately known as KGs. It wasn't the best neighborhood, but it was home and had birthed some of the most thoroughbred men and women in Kansas City.

"Who she know from my hood? Let me find out lil' sis 'bout that life."

"Hell nah, she ain't," Synovi replied smoothly. "She ain't got no reason to be over there."

"Shit, she might. Might meet her a real nigga." Tae chuckled.

"Yeah, a'ight."

Synovi didn't doubt for one second that Racquel was on good bullshit having him come pick her up. He just hoped niggas didn't get out of line when he showed up because Synovi wasn't in the mood, but he'd check shit behind Racquel if it came down to it. Ditzy and reckless with the way she moved or not, she changed his life for the better, and Synovi vowed to try his best to keep her safe.

The scowl on Racquel's face deepened as the blunt being exchanged from one hand to another passed in front of her. Waving the smoke from her view, she sucked her teeth. Having just gotten her hair shampooed and curled the day before, she knew she'd be right back in Moo's chair after today. The potent stench of weed clung to her entire being, and she was fed up.

"Yo' uppity ass need to hit the blunt, and maybe you'll relax," Khysen, one of the young hustlers, told her.

"I'm fine," Racquel grumbled.

Khysen shrugged and inhaled the smoke before slowly blowing it out. "Shit, more for us."

Gone was her bubbly personality and contagious smile. While trying to enjoy her summer break, she figured hanging out with a few friends who claimed to miss her wouldn't hurt. Her first mistake was agreeing to kick it, not knowing where they were going. The second mistake was not driving her car. Had she, Racquel would've been gone long before now.

"I can't believe they just left us here," Lakisha, Racquel's friend, said.

They had met at school, found out they were from the same city, and had been hanging out ever since. This was their first time kicking it together back home, and Racquel was mad that it was inside what she knew was a trap house. At least, that was what it resembled to her. She wasn't quite sure.

Her friends Kaela and Mya had gone to the store with promises to return. That was over thirty minutes ago, and neither had answered their phones when she called to see where they were.

"And they're not answering the phone. That's okay," Racquel mumbled, nodding her head. "I'm good on them."

"You better mean it this time, too. What kind of friends bring you somewhere and dip out? That's shady as fuck," Lakisha sneered. "I'd cut a bitch off for being on that type of time. Or beat her ass."

Racquel was far from a fighter, but if she decided to become one, laying hands on Kaela and Mya would be warranted. This wasn't the first time either of them had done shady, conniving things to her, but Racquel vowed it'd be the last. In a sense, her first year of college had matured her, but her lack of discernment was still present.

The bass from the obnoxiously loud rap music coming from the floor speaker rattled her nerves while she and Lakisha sipped on a mixed drink from red Solo cups. Though they hadn't brought their own bottle, a brand-new bottle of tequila had been opened in front of them. Lakisha had to remind Racquel not to drink from anything she didn't see a seal on or be poured. They weren't of age to be drinking in the first place; getting drugged was the last thing they needed to happen. None of the men in the apartment were on that type of time, so they had nothing to worry about.

"What y'all in a rush to leave for?" Khysen questioned.

Glancing at the men crouched on the kitchen tile, shooting dice, Racquel had to admit that they were handsome and had been respectful since they arrived. The guns, money, and drugs everywhere were partially why she wanted to shake the scene. Her attitude being on ten was the main reason, though. Once she was annoyed, which hardly occurred, there was no understanding with her.

"This isn't my vibe," Racquel voiced.

Khysen looked to Lakisha for a response.

"I rode here with her, so if she's ready to go, we're leaving together."

His head bobbed upward once. "Solid. Those other girls left y'all asses, huh?"

His light chuckle made Racquel's crabby mood simmer some, but her eyes still rolled. "Let's not state the obvious."

Before Khysen could say anything else, Racquel's phone rang with an incoming call from Synovi.

"Hello?" she answered.

"Yeah. I think I'm outside. What building is it?"

Racquel looked over at Khysen. "What building number is this?"

"F."

Racquel recited the letter and stood from the couch. Lakisha did the same after taking another sip of her drink.

"Let me walk y'all down," Khysen said, seemingly having manners suddenly.

Racquel eyed him as she adjusted her crossbody purse. “Aren’t you the same person who said I can’t have someone pull up over here, and now you want to walk us out? Please.” She smirked and waved him off.

Khysen shot her a grin as he walked behind them to the door.

“I am. Gotta make sure y’all not on no sneaky shit.”

That was the least of their worries. Once they made it outside, Racquel spotted Synovi’s Tahoe right away. Her eyes squinted as the passenger door opened, and Tae hopped out.

“Nigga, what you doing with my boss’s lil’ sister?” Tae inquired as he walked up to Khysen. Slapping hands, they dapped one another up.

“The better question is, what she doing over here.” Khysen laughed.

The two young men ran in the same crew and had been friends since they were kids. KGs was their stomping grounds.

“Nothing now,” Racquel answered as she moseyed by them.

“Damn, you can’t say bye? Drank up all my liquor and gon’ just slide out, huh?” Khysen joked, eyeing her slim, fit frame in the leggings she had on.

Racquel had been warned about gaining the freshman fifteen weight in her first year of undergrad, and she had underestimated the warnings. Between eating at the student union with eight different restaurant options, the two dining halls, and drinking liquor like a fish, Racquel had thickened up nicely. All the walking she did on campus kept it proportioned, with her thighs nice and toned, but now she knew hitting the recreation center next semester would be in her plans if she wanted to keep her stomach flat.

"She ain't speak to a nigga either. What's good?" Tae spoke.

In a much better mood now that she was out of the stuffy, smoke-filled apartment, Racquel gave them both a genuine smile. Addressing Tae first, she said, "Hey." Focusing on Khysen, she admired his handsome, smooth, chocolate baby face. Now that they were out in the sunlight, she couldn't help but notice how clear his skin was. Nor could she ignore his crisp hairline and juicy lips.

"See you around. Thanks for being so hospitable," Racquel said with a smirk.

Khysen licked his lips. "No problem at all, gorgeous."

Tae chuckled and gave Lakisha a head nod. "What's up, Kish?"

"Not a thing. I didn't know you knew Racquel."

"I'ont know her like that. I work for her people's nem," Tae expressed.

"That's what's up. Small world. We go to school together."

Tae liked the sound of that. "Yeah? I'ma have to make that drive to see y'all."

Lakisha laughed. "Yeah, okay, boy. Imagine that. Let me get in this truck. Thanks for sharing your blunt," she said to Khysen.

He acknowledged her gratitude with an upward head bob.

"You on that?" Tae asked.

"Nah, I wasn't, but shit, which one?"

The friends laughed. Unbeknownst to Khysen, Tae found Racquel fine as hell. She popped up at the job a few times, and of course, he introduced himself. He followed her Instagram page, but that was as far as it went. Today, he had other plans unless his boy did too.

"You tryna see which one on go?" Tae speculated.

Khysen shook his head no. He'd come across a bunch of thirsty, down to fuck females in his life. Based on some of their conversation alone, Khysen knew which ones would readily give the pussy up without much thought. Racquel and Lakisha weren't that type at all.

"Nah. I'd get on Racquel, though. It's something about her," Khysen mused.

Their eyes were transfixed on her as she pulled the passenger door open. Their interests were piqued, but Tae knew he couldn't make any moves now, knowing she and Lakisha were friends. He used to be in a serious relationship with one of Lakisha's cousins and knew where her loyalty lay. Pushing up on Racquel in any capacity around her wouldn't be going down, so he let the idea of having her go.

"Yeah, it definitely is. Good luck with that, my boy," he said, patting Khysen's chest twice with the back of his hand.

Racquel shut the passenger door with a huff and then smiled at Synovi. "Hey."

He shook his head. "You ain't gon' learn."

"Whaaat?" she whined, knowing he was about to go in on her. "It's not my fault the people I rode with left me."

"Nah, it ain't, but they shouldn't have had the chance to play you like that. You got yo' homegirl with you, so I'ma leave the situation alone for now," he said.

Racquel was thankful for that. As cool as she and Lakisha were, she didn't want her to witness him scolding her for lack of discernment. Something Lakisha had preached to her all semester long. Some of the choices she made early on in the school year were questionable, but lessons she needed to learn.

"Thank you," Racquel mumbled. "This my homegirl Kish. Kish, this is my sister's boyfriend, Synovi."

"Hey," Lakisha spoke.

Synovi glanced at her through the rearview. "What up. Nice to meet you." He rolled his window down. "If you not trying to get left, you need to come on," he said to Tae.

"I'm still on the clock. You can't leave me." Tae laughed.

Synovi shifted gears, and Tae's eyes widened, seeing the red brake lights. He and Khysen cracked up laughing.

"Aye. That man bouta skate out," Khysen said as he and Tae slapped hands.

"Hell yeah. I'ma catch you niggas when I get off."

He walked the short distance to the truck and was about to hop inside when a black Acura swooped into the parking lot like they were on a high-speed chase. Tae's hand went to the gun on his waist. The windows were tinted, so he couldn't see inside, but he'd be a fool to get caught lacking. When two women stepped out, his top lip curled upward.

"Y'all need to slow that piece of shit down, driving through here," he hissed.

Kaela waved him off. "Boy, whatever. What y'all doing outside? Everybody left?"

"Girl, look who finally showed back up," Lakisha said from the back seat.

Racquel sucked her teeth. "I'm about to say something," she said, pushing the door back open.

"Aye," Synovi called out. "I ain't trying to be here all day. I got shit to do."

She grinned. "I'll make it quick. Promise."

Lakisha opened her door as well. She didn't know Kaela or Mya, but she knew Racquel. Whatever she was about to say was going to piss them off, and she wanted to be right by her side.

"Oop. Not y'all were about to leave," Mya jested, seeing them emerge.

"Yeah, like y'all left us. That's not coo' at all," Racquel said.

Kaela rolled her eyes. "Girl, I told you we were coming right back. You didn't have to call somebody to come get you. That's the shit I be talking about."

"What shit? Please, enlighten me," Racquel urged, cocking her head to the side.

"Acting like you too fucking good to be somewhere and always complaining. If I said we'd be right back, you didn't need to blow our phones up. I thought bringing you around some real niggas would help you not be so fucking green, but I guess not." Kaela laughed as Mya shook her head with a smirk.

"I never said I was too good to be anywhere. And

how is wanting to know where y'all at complaining? Make it make sense," Racquel said.

"Nah. I'm good. Gon' 'head and leave like y'all were going to do," Kaela replied.

Lakisha stepped their way. "For one, ain't no real bitch gon' leave her friend somewhere by herself when she came with y'all. Luckily, I was here with her. Green or not, you hoes are weird."

"Hoes!" Mya screeched.

"Yeah. Some fake ass hoes," Lakisha said sternly. "Don't fake like you're friends with her for real."

Kaela looked at Racquel. "You gon' let her call us out of our name like that?"

"She didn't lie. What y'all did was fake, and I think it's best if we not be friends anymore."

Mya laughed. "Girl, okay."

"Right," Kaela added. "You went off to college and think you better than everybody now? Got you some new friends and think you all that. Okay, girl. Hopefully, they can give you some lessons on fixing that trauma bonding issue you have."

White noise surrounded Racquel, drowning out all rational thoughts. As a friend, she confided in Kaela about almost everything, as one would do with their friends. Yet, she stood there with not an ounce of care for a subject Racquel struggled with. Throwing something she shared in her face publicly had Racquel seeing red.

In haste, she was across the sidewalk and crazily swinging at Kaela. The anger and hurt she was experiencing made her chest tight and punches vicious. Kaela was so caught off guard, she could hardly get any hits in before Racquel was being pulled off her.

"You so weak for that!" Mya fussed, rushing to her friend's side.

"Fuck both of y'all!" Racquel shouted.

Her eyes brimmed with angry tears and seared with hatred like no other. Had Khysen not been holding onto her trembling frame, he was sure she'd crumble. Pulling her away from the scrutiny of the neighbors who wanted to see what was going on, Khysen carried her to the truck. Synovi met them at the edge of the sidewalk. Tae and Lakisha were right behind them.

"I let you out of my sight for two minutes, and you fighting?" Synovi sighed.

Khysen glanced his way. "Aye, not right now. I know you her people and shit, but let her chill for a second."

He wasn't asking Synovi; he told him. Pulling the passenger door open, Khysen sat her in the seat. Her leg bounced as she squeezed her eyes shut. So many crazy scenarios floated through her mind, Racquel had to will herself not to hop back out and go berserk again. She couldn't believe Kaela had the nerve to go that low.

Then again, she should've known not to expect much from someone who talked shit about her but mimicked everything she did. It was so disheartening, and Racquel hated how exposed she felt at the moment.

"Yo, Rocky... you not gon' hop out once I move, are you?" Khysen questioned.

Racquel peeled her eyes open. "Rocky?"

He lightly smirked. "Yeah. That's what I'ma call you

from now on. You were throwing punches like you've been in the ring."

She wanted to show some type of reaction to the impromptu nickname he'd given her, but the only emotion festering at the moment was anger. Pure disgust. Assessing his proximity as he stood between her legs, Racquel swallowed hard. Regardless of what had just gone down, she couldn't ignore the heat of his body or his protectiveness. It was overwhelming, to say the least. Peeping her lingering eyes, Khysen took a step back.

"My bad," he mumbled.

"It's fine." She cleared her throat. "I'm okay, though. Just blacked out for a second."

Khysen nodded. "Sometimes you have to so a motha-fucka knows not to play with you anymore."

They locked eyes, and Racquel hated how her insides swirled under his intense gaze. Those dark brown orbs of his lingered with solicitous questioning. Racquel didn't want to make Khysen privy to the questions she knew he had.

"True." Racquel sighed.

Uncertain if she was supposed to thank him for removing her from the situation or not, she focused her attention on Synovi, who stood off to the side. He, too, had a few questions.

"You good, friend?" Lakisha asked.

Racquel nodded. "Yeah. We can leave now."

In the distance, Kaela and Mya yelled obscenities about her having to see them again, but Racquel paid them no mind. The damage, mentally for her and physically to Kaela's face, was already done.

"You should've let her get some more licks in," Tae said.

"Shut up, fool. She don't need to be out here fighting and shit. Too damn pretty for that. Ol' girl deserved it, though," Khysen said.

Synovi couldn't help but agree. Still, he was proud of her for standing up for herself. He didn't know what had been said for her to start swinging, but whatever it was had to be serious.

"You getting in the back?" Synovi asked, watching her pull the back door open.

Everyone watched her as if she were a child who needed to be looked after.

"Yeah. I don't wanna take Tae's spot."

"Nah, you good. Unless you just wanna sit with your friend," Tae joked, lightening the mood.

In fact, that was what Racquel wanted to do. She wasn't ready for the questioning she knew Synovi had. They piled into the truck, and Khysen lingered by her door once it was closed. Noticing him still standing there, Racquel rolled her window down.

"Yes?" she asked nicely.

"Let me know when you make it home."

"And how do you suppose I do that?"

Khysen licked his lips and backed away from the truck. "You seem like a smart girl. I'm sure you'll figure it out."

That got a smile out of her. A visual Khysen enjoyed witnessing more than the unpleasant frown she'd sported almost the entire time she was in his presence. When Synovi pulled out of the complex, Racquel sighed and rested her head against the seat. It was still early in the day and had already felt longer than it should've.

Never did she think coming home and trying to maintain the friendships she hardly had would lead to this. Kaela's words triggered her to no end, and the unresolved trauma she was trying her best to deal with came to a head. There was only so much more she could take with it now on the surface.

"Y'all going to your mama's?" Synovi asked.

Racquel pulled her eyes away from the window. "Yeah."

He nodded and headed toward Ms. Tracee's house. Racquel couldn't wait to get home. Not because she wanted to tell her mama what happened but because she could be alone with her thoughts and cry in peace. For years, that'd been her way of self-soothing, and now, she wondered if isolating herself would be enough to get her through.

two

"Now, where else you say you were going?" GiGi asked as Torin turned into her parking lot.

"I have to go to one more store, and then I'm going home. Well, to Novi's place," Torin answered.

The duo had been out almost all day, running in and out of stores. GiGi called while Torin was doing a breakfast drop-off, wanting to know if she could run her a few places. It was nothing for Torin to swoop GiGi up for a girls's day, take her to handle business, or even go sit and relax with her. Their relationship had grown closer than she thought it would, and she was so grateful for their bond.

"Y'all might as well gon' 'head and move in together. You're always over there," GiGi said.

Torin snickered. "It's too soon, plus I like my house."

"Y'all can get a home and *like* it together," GiGi insisted.

She couldn't help but laugh as she placed the gear in park. "Okay, GiGi. I'ma ask him and see what he says."

"You already know what he's going to say. He thinks he's the boss, but it's always, *Whatever Love wants. Let me see what Love says.*"

The way she mimicked Synovi's voice made Torin cackle. Synovi made it abundantly clear that when it came to drastic decision-making, Torin's opinion mattered. She'd been the voice of reason behind most of his business ventures and life adjustments thus far. So, yes, it was whatever Love said, but Torin knew her man.

His independence was something he cherished and appreciated. For so long, he had nothing to call his own, so sharing a home so soon wasn't ideal. The young boy in him was living the dreams he never thought would become a reality. Torin didn't want to interfere with that, only add to it.

"He values my opinion, GiGi." Torin snickered, unclicking her seatbelt.

"Mhm. I know he does. That's a good thing. I'd be telling you to run in the other direction if he didn't."

"Well, thankfully, I don't have to worry about that. You raised a good man."

GiGi smiled brightly. "I did my best, baby. Lord knows I prayed so hard for him. On days when I didn't know what to pray for, I just thanked Him for keeping Synovi. To soften his heart and let people in to love him. It took some time, but He came on through. Now look at him. Can't even bring his tail over here on Sundays like he used to. Your cooking ain't all that, missy," GiGi fake fussed, pushing her door open.

Giggling, Torin did the same. "Oooh. Don't let me find out you hating on me."

"Child, please. There's not one hater bone in my body. You better ask about me."

If GiGi didn't do anything else, she would have Torin's jaws and stomach hurting from laughing so much. They carried her groceries in through the main entrance, running into Carolynn on the way to her apartment.

"Hey, Ms. Carolynn. How are you?" Torin spoke.

"I'm doing all right. I see y'all done been out shopping and left me here."

GiGi scoffed. "You weren't invited."

"Oh, don't tell me you're still upset about the Spades game from the other night," Carolynn said, following them down the hall.

"I sure as hell am. Should've never sat in that chair if you didn't come to play. Made me look crazy," GiGi fussed.

Amused, Torin shook her head. "Y'all loss every game?"

"No. Just one. You know how she gets, honey. Be fussing for no reason," Carolynn concluded.

This Torin knew. It was comical seeing the friends bicker every week over this and that. Yet, they were always together when Torin came to visit.

"I fuss 'cause I can. You can make it all better if you fix me a caramel cake."

Carolynn bumped Torin's shoulder and pursed her lips. "Mhm. Sure. I'll have to get the ingredients."

"Oh, don't worry about those. I picked everything up when we were out. They're in one of these Walmart bags."

"She just knew I'd be fixing her a cake," Carolynn whispered to Torin.

"What was that?" GiGi questioned.

They both giggled as she continued putting things away. When Torin was positive GiGi didn't need her assistance anymore, she used the bathroom before preparing to leave.

"Don't forget what we talked about, my girl," GiGi said, holding the front door open.

Torin smiled and leaned in to hug her. "I won't. Call me later on this week."

"You know I will. Drive safely."

Torin left GiGi's in such a good mood. She wanted to say forget about making her last store run, but she needed more vanilla extract. Thankfully, the grocery store by his condo had some.

Within ten minutes, she was in and out of the store with the item she came for, plus a few other things. It wouldn't be her if she hadn't found something else she needed to grab.

The giddy smile on her face couldn't be contained as she pulled into his driveway and opened the garage door. His truck was backed in its usual spot on the left, leaving Torin space on the right. They hadn't spoken since earlier in the day, and she couldn't wait to love up on him.

Hearing the garage open, Synovi made his way out to help her. Regardless of whether Torin said she wasn't going to buy anything while out with GiGi, she always came home with shopping bags. Like the dutiful man of hers he was, Synovi was right there to carry them into the house.

With the phone perched on his ear, he grinned and smooched her lips. "What's up, Love? Yeah, my lady just got home. Nah, nah. We're good. Run those days by me again."

Entranced, Torin's eyes filled with desire as he grabbed bags out of the backseat. While he did so, Torin took that opportunity to admire him. The white tank top he wore showcased his recent love for the gym. Bulging, tattooed arms flexed as he maneuvered every bag into his grasp.

Ogling him momentarily paralyzed her as she imagined Synovi hovering above her while sliding that dick deep in her. Catching a chill, she shivered and softly chuckled before snapping out of her daydream. Synovi gave her a puzzled glance, and she just smirked before following him inside the house.

Continuing his phone conversation, Synovi headed inside the second bedroom they'd converted into an office space while Torin put the groceries away. This was their routine on most weekdays. Business and work were handled during business hours, and then they made time for each other. Synovi didn't necessarily have to stay at the office all day or go in half the time, but he enjoyed it. Waking up and walking into a successful business he grinded for, kept him grounded.

Torin's schedule, on the other hand, wasn't as consistent. Being a chef came with crazy hours, but she was used to it. Over the last seven months, her workload and clientele had increased tremendously, and she was beyond grateful. This year, she planned on taking Kaine's Kitchen to a new level.

Peeking her head inside the office, she noticed Synovi still handling business on his iMac. Walking over to him, she placed his favorite candy she'd picked up at the store on the desk. His confused, semi-shocked expression always reminded her of the trauma he endured growing up. Synovi was raised on survival, while Torin was raised on love.

She'd picked up on the distinction early on in their friendship, but especially after the day party last year. Their upbringing didn't necessarily mean either would conform to what society thought they should, but it played a huge role in the growth of their relationship.

Cognizant of certain things, something as simple as Torin bringing him his favorite candy felt transactional, even though Synovi knew those weren't her intentions. She wanted nothing in return and never would. Being with a woman like Torin forced Synovi to unlearn what he thought was healthy and adapt to having a more positive outlook on life.

In the beginning, it wasn't easy accepting the love Torin openly showered him with. He didn't understand it, but he had no choice but to. Synovi's resilience thus far proved his determination to continue nourishing the healthy, loving environment he never thought he'd be in. An appreciative smile graced his face as he faced her. It was an expression he had easily provided since Torin entered his life.

His hand glided up the back of her thigh before squeezing her ass. *Thank you*, he mouthed before picking up the pack of peanut M&M's and returning to his call. The small things she did made Synovi love her even more. Shit she knew would make his day better. Her thoughtfulness and consideration for him hadn't wavered a bit.

Seeing him log in to the scheduling app was her cue to go, so she let him be and headed upstairs. She wanted to get out of her clothes and into something more comfy for the evening. As GiGi said, Torin practically lived at Synovi's place. It used to be the other way around when they first met, but she found herself at his home more nights than her own. Adding her personal touch and coziness to his condo had a lot to do with that.

Entering his bedroom, Torin stopped in her tracks. Her cheeks lifted, and her eyes squinted in wonderment, noticing the Nordstrom bags on the bed. A fresh vase of flowers sat on the nightstand on her side of the bed. Synovi hadn't mentioned anything about going to the mall when they spoke earlier. Unlike Torin, who couldn't keep anything she got him a secret, Synovi kept her *I just wanna buy you something* gifts under wraps.

This wasn't the first time she'd come home to new things, and her appreciation for them never lessened. Even when he wasn't in a position to splurge on her financially, Synovi had been an attentive lover. Spoiling her on a random weekday just to see that smile on her face was all he wanted to do.

Cheesing extra hard, Torin went through the first bag. Her heart couldn't help but melt when she saw the cream Double T Tory Burch fluffy slippers. With Synovi having wood floors throughout the condo, Torin's feet stayed cold.

It was nothing for him to grab her a pair of socks

from his drawer, but having her own set of house shoes seemed like the better option, so he copped her some. Two pairs, actually. Wanting her to have options, Synovi bought a pair of suede UGG slippers as well.

"I know that's right." She beamed, reaching inside the last bag.

Pulling out a red silk robe and a black cotton one, Torin couldn't help but get emotional. It was one thing for her man to listen to her, but to take action after one of their late-night talks in bed, was why Torin was never coming up off him.

They hypothetically discussed what their lives would be like had they not been entrepreneurs, and Torin stated she'd be put up in a nice, modest home, draped in floor-length silk robes, preparing meals for her husband and children while sipping a glass of wine, and living the best soft life possible.

That was a fairytale dream, though. She couldn't fathom that being her reality with her work ethic. She had so many goals to accomplish, and it wasn't quite time for that role yet. In his mind, she deserved that now, if even a glimpse. Synovi felt honored to provide his woman with a life of ease and comfort. A woman who selflessly made his life worth living.

Stepping over to the bouquet of pink tulips, she plucked the small pink envelope attached to the vase. A smile lifted her cheeks as she read over the note.

I hope you had a good day, Love.

His words were simple yet beyond sweet. Conveyed in only a way Synovi could. Her day had been good, and she was about to make his even better. With a pep in her step, determined to let him know how thankful she was for him, Torin practically skipped down the steps in her new footwear and into his office.

Discreetly, though Synovi felt her presence before she entered the room, Torin stood behind him at his desk. She ran a hand over his soft, black waves and kissed the tattoo aligning his crisp line while massaging his shoulders. Her hands trailed down his pecs as she peppered kisses along his neck. Inhaling, she savored his fresh scent, and her mouth watered, knowing he tasted just as good.

To confirm what she already knew, Torin licked his neck slowly. "Mmm." She hummed softly.

Synovi let her feel him up until she stuck her hand inside the band of his jogger shorts to caress his dick. He cleared his throat and swiveled his chair, so he was facing her. A mischievous grin teased the corners of her mouth.

"A'ight. One-thirty on Thursday. Don't forget; I'm not giving you a reminder," he told Tae before ending the call.

It was the last business-related call he was taking for the evening, and he made sure of it by turning his ringer off. Sliding the phone on his desk, Synovi focused on the beauty before him. His heart constricted with pride, and his dick stiffened seeing the content smile on her face. *She's happy*, he said to himself.

"I see someone went shopping," Torin said.

Synovi looked down at her fuzzy-covered feet. "You like them?"

"I love them," she acknowledged, kissing his lips. "And I love you. Thank you, baby."

When she lowered to her knees, Synovi's thick brows dipped. Not out of confusion because he knew exactly what she was about to bless him with, but because he wanted to tell her the news he'd just gotten.

"Hol' up. I need to tell you something."

She stroked him through his shorts, urging him to lower them and his briefs. "I have to tell him something, too," she cooed.

Torin wanted to slide his dick so far down her throat that all she tasted was him for the rest of the day. Fuck the dinner she planned on cooking. Relinquishing some of his dominance and bossy personality, Synovi let her do her thing. Teasingly, Torin kissed around the tip, swirling her tongue thrice.

"Love." Synovi groaned.

That was the only warning he was giving her to stop playing and swallow his dick. Torin snickered before doing just that. She sucked him into her warm, wet mouth and didn't come up for air until spittle dripped onto the carpeted area. Synovi's low grunts encouraged her to go harder. His right eye twitched, and his nostrils flared as she took him down her throat.

"Shiiit," Synovi hissed. "Eat that dick up, Love."

She planned to do that anyway, and his disgruntled request only made her want to please him more. Under the scrutiny of his dark orbs filled with adoration, Torin got downright nasty with it. His knuckles were damn near white from the grip he had on the armrests. He tried to maintain eye contact but failed when Torin moaned like sucking his dick was made for her enjoyment only.

"Mmm, hmm." She hummed.

The vibrations made his toes pop. Feeling him tense up, Torin bobbed her head quickly. Up and down, she worked her jaws with determination.

"Slow down," Synovi huffed, gripping a handful of her braids. "Yeeeah, like that. Just like that. Fuck!"

Torin's unrushed movements provided a different level of pleasure. Slow and steady did win the race, and she was in competition with herself. Synovi's throaty groans were all the encouragement she needed. Craving to pull that nut up out of him, she toyed with his balls before sucking on his tip and using both hands to stroke him. Her palms twisting in opposite directions made Synovi stand from his chair.

"You so damn pretty sucking my dick." He moaned lowly.

Her lashes fluttered as she smiled up at him. Widening his stance, Synovi thrust his hips, keeping the pace until his impending nut surfaced. In pure ecstasy, Torin gagged, and before he could stop himself, Synovi was nutting down her throat. His entire body stiffened as he watched her swallow every drop and lick her lips. With a heaving chest and blurred vision, Synovi fell into the chair.

"C'mere." He panted, pulling her upward and to him before she had a chance to.

With urgency, Synovi's lips met hers, and they shared a sloppy tongue kiss. When he went to unbuckle her pants, Torin smirked and pulled away from him.

"What's the matter?" he questioned, concern lacing his tone.

"What were you going to tell me?"

Confused, Synovi looked down at his dick and then back up at her. "I told you to come here."

"No, before that. You said you had to tell me something, but I had other plans."

"Obviously," he mumbled, standing to pull his briefs and shorts up before sitting back down.

He made a mental reminder to disinfect his chair before he left his office. His head tilted to the side as he rummaged through his brain for the information she asked for.

"You are too young not to remember something from ten minutes ago," Torin jested.

Synovi licked his lips. "If you hadn't come in here and sucked my thoughts away, I could think straight."

Giggling, Torin sat on his lap. "Oh, whatever. Don't blame me. Let's jog your memory."

"I'd much rather slide in some pussy, but a'ight."

She couldn't help but laugh at the serious expression on his face. Torin was trying to have a full-blown conversation at the wrong time.

"You had a bunch of phone calls," she stated.

"Yeah. No matter how much I try to leave work at work, it never ends up that way. I ain't complaining, though. Oh, damn. That's what it was," he said, a hint of excitement in his voice.

Torin perked up. "What?"

"We both made it to the finals for the awards."

Torin's eyes widened. "What!" she screeched, hopping up. "We did? I didn't even know. Oh, my gosh, Novi! That's huge. I'm so proud of you."

She threw herself at him, hugging him tightly. Synovi's chest swelled with pride hearing the emotion in her voice. He hugged her back and cleared his throat.

"I'm proud of you, too. Like crazy. You've been putting in work, and it's paying off."

When the Kansas City's People's Choice Awards semi-finalists list was first posted, Synovi and Torin were both shocked to see that they'd been advanced to the next level. Neither of them had a clue people had nominated their businesses, and they were beyond grateful.

Their loyal clientele had held it down during the voting periods without them having to do much, which spoke highly of their services.

The annual ceremony hosted by Terrell Ray honored and celebrated the excellence and achievements of organizations, small businesses, and entrepreneurs throughout Kansas City. The vision to pay homage to the community leaders and influencers in 2019 had expanded to a city and state-known event and had become a staple in the community.

As a young, Black businessman trying to make a name for himself, Synovi was honored to be listed alongside some greats from his city. Torin being one of them. Despite the drama that'd surrounded her name last year with Jade's messy antics, it didn't interfere with Kaine's Kitchen. In fact, it made those who hadn't tried her food see what the fuss was all about.

Now, Kaine's Kitchen was sitting on a list with some of the coldest chefs known to have the best food and catering services in the city. Torin was positive that if she'd reacted that early morning the way she wanted to, things wouldn't have been the same. Thankfully, Synovi hadn't let her. Jeopardizing her brand and all she'd worked hard for over some lies wasn't something he would ever allow.

"It really is. But, look at SB's! You haven't been in business a full year, and you're already making noise. I know that's fucking right. Tell them to put some respect on your name."

Torin hit the chicken head dance, making Synovi chuckle. He never needed a hype man; she was it.

"We attending?" he asked, and her movements halted.

"Of course, we are. You don't want to? We're finalists, baby."

He knew that. It'd be more than a good look if he went and represented, but something was hindering him. Synovi hadn't fully come to grips with the life he was living. While inspiring, the roles he had to fill were intimidating as well.

Some days, he relished in the fact that he bounced back and overcame so much, and other days, impostor syndrome choked him out. The bitch had hands for sure, and Synovi was tired of swinging back.

"Yeah, I know. It just seems unreal that this is my life."

Torin got all in his face. "But it is, and I'ma need you to start acting like it. You made that list because you deserve to be on there. Starting a cleaning service, a reputable one at that, isn't easy. Your clients and whomever else voted for you to win because they believe in you. They trust you. Whether they did or not, you and I both know what SB brings to the table. I'ma need you to stop playing small and stand on all that big boss shit you're made of. 'Cause if not, we're gonna have some problems, sir."

The way she stood before him with that hip poked out, and arms crossed made his dick hard and heart wide the fuck open. With her, he could let his guard down and be vulnerable. Synovi didn't mind lying his insecurities on display for Torin to assess and reassure. She coddled his emotions with the utmost genuine sternness, leaving him room to grow but not bask in the uncertainty of who he wasn't.

"Some problems, huh?" Synovi mused. "I'ont want no problems with you, Love."

"I know you don't. I get it... This is all new for you, but trust me, God wouldn't have you here if you weren't supposed to be. You thought He brought you this far just for you to play in His face?"

Synovi chuckled. "Man, ain't nobody doing that. A nigga just surprised, that's all."

"No lie." Torin giggled. "I am, too. I can't believe I made it, but this isn't about me."

"But it is, though. SBCS wouldn't be what it is today without you. I be in my head a lot, questioning why or how, but you remain patient with me. Keep a nigga away from them tunnels. My win is your win, so I'ma start moving like it."

Smiling, Torin retook her spot on his lap. "I love that for us," she said, kissing his lips.

"I bet you do." He chuckled, rubbing up and down her thighs. "Can we get back to what we were doing?"

He asked but was already fiddling with the button of her pants. Synovi wasn't about to let her sit all that ass in his lap and not do anything with it.

"Wait," she voiced, gripping his wrist. "We need to share the voting links and stuff to our social media pages and email lists."

Synovi gave her a deadpan stare. "I'm off the clock, Love. The only thing I feel like sharing is this dick and you acting like you don't want it. In a second, I'ma just bend you over this desk; fuck waiting."

Bossy ass.

His calm, yearning tone made her nipples pebble and pussy wetter. Torin didn't need him to say another word. Doing the honors, she stood and unbuttoned her pants. The slight struggle she had getting them over her ass amused him, but Synovi loved the show. He admired her thick, caramel frame, wondering where on her body she'd get his name tatted. Synovi knew where he'd get hers if she asked. He'd make room for it right over his heart because she had the mothafucka on lock. When she went to remove her thong, Synovi pulled her to him by the thin black fabric.

"Keep this on," he said huskily, guiding her onto his lap.

Torin wasn't sure when he'd lowered his shorts and briefs, but the head of his dick greeted her opening before he was fully submerged by her wetness. She lost her breath at his intrusion.

"Ugh! You're so deeeep," Torin moaned, creaming his pole while bracing herself on his desk.

The arch in her back and sexy moans had him ready to act a fool in it.

Widening his seated position, Synovi spread her cheeks open, exposing her pretty pink center, gripping him tightly. He groaned at the sight and gave her ass a smack. He wasn't trying to hear anything she was saying unless she was moaning his name.

"Good. You need to feel all this dick," he asserted.

Leaning over her, Synovi licked up her spine and kissed her shoulder before whispering in her ear. "Congratulations, baby. Now throw that ass back, and you better not run."

Now that she could do. The no-running part was still up for debate.

three

Sitting in the passenger seat of Synovi's truck, Torin shook her head as she listened to Racquel grope over the phone. As much as she complained about being back home, she just knew her little sister would be returning to school earlier than planned.

"So, what do you think?" Racquel sighed dramatically.

"I think you need to stay in the dorms for another year like we discussed. Enjoy the experience with your roommates. That's why you're in the leadership program, to begin with. What's the point of rushing to get an apartment and take on more responsibilities? Bills, I know you're going to call me complaining about it," Torin said.

She didn't understand it. For someone who received scholarships to cover room and board, Torin found it foolish for Racquel to want to up and get an apartment. Calling for her advice was only going to piss Racquel off because she wasn't pacifying her feelings.

"Just forget it," Racquel mumbled. "You're always going to be on Mommy's side."

"That's not true," Torin defended. "You don't like hearing my opinion because you know I'm not going to sugarcoat it, but you still ask me for that very reason. It doesn't make sense for you to move off campus like Mommy said, but I guess you'll learn the hard way if that's what you decide to do."

Racquel huffed on the other end. "I have about a month to decide."

"Which isn't hardly enough time, Racquel."

"It is! I already started looking at apartments before I came home."

Torin was over the conversation for now. Getting her to see where she was coming from was of no use. It was bad enough that Torin had no idea about the incident a few weeks ago when Synovi picked her up. Racquel asked him not to tell her what had gone down. He hadn't yet, and she hoped it stayed that way.

"Okay," was all Torin had to say before she snapped. "I'm about to get my nails done, so I'll call you when I leave."

"Dang. You couldn't ask if I wanted to come with you?"

Laughing, Torin said, "You got nail money? You need to be saving every dime for that apartment you want that I'm sure costs a grip."

"You really get on my nerves. Bye!"

"Bye, girl," Torin said before the line disconnected. "I'm not about to let her stress me out. Move into her own apartment for what? What's the rush? She needs to be focused on her grades and figuring out what field she wants to major in. I know for a fact there are already enough things distracting her. Moving off campus will only lead to more."

Synovi listened intently while pulling into the parking lot where Moo's shop was located. Her frustration was warranted, but Synovi needed her to do something for him.

"Relax, Love."

Those two words spoken so gently blanketed her nerves, eliminating them immediately. Whenever she got to rambling about things out of her control, Synovi reeled her in. He hated seeing her overwhelmed, and any chance he could alleviate some of the pressure, he would. With her posture loosened, jaw unclenched, and a deep exhale, Torin followed his commands like a well-versed scholar.

"I said I wasn't going to let her stress me out and look at me." She chuckled.

"You big sis. It's inevitable not to. She'll learn it's all out of love, though. Gotta let her figure some shit out on her own."

Torin didn't want her to take that route, but she would end the conversation for now.

"You're right. What time are you supposed to be meeting Candace?" she questioned, using Ms. Reid's first name.

Eyeing the clock, he responded, "In ten minutes. We right on time."

Although he no longer lived at Solace Place, Synovi still linked up with Ms. Reid once or twice a month to check in. Normally, when you left the program, you'd receive outreach services. In Synovi's case, since he was terminated for fighting, those services weren't readily offered to him. Ms. Reid wasn't going for that, though. It didn't matter to her that she wasn't the outreach coordinator.

She'd witnessed his progress over the year she'd counseled him and felt it was her responsibility to make sure he followed through with his goals. Synovi could proudly say each of the goals he'd written down when they first connected had been met and scratched off. Now, he had others to accomplish.

"Okay, good. What color should I get my nails?"

Torin couldn't keep them long due to her profession, but she loved getting them done when she could. Her go-to almond shape was short and perfect. Synovi wasn't sure which color to choose, but he was used to her wanting his opinion, so he gave it.

"Nude," he replied. "Isn't that the color you told me you like?"

Torin nodded with a smirk. "Mhm."

"Get the white tips on your toes. I like when you get that, too."

She blushed embarrassingly hard but didn't shy away from his smoldering gaze. Torin had an intense urge to start some shit she knew she couldn't finish right then, so she kept her salacious comments to herself. Knowing Synovi, he'd turn her every way but loose in that truck, forcing them to both reschedule their plans.

"I didn't know you liked it when I got French tips," Torin stated.

"You should. That's when I lick on them the most."

His Cheshire grin proved that he knew exactly how his words affected her. Torin's center throbbed, and she shook her head while unlatching her seatbelt.

"Duly noted. Let me get in here before I have you licking on something else." She giggled, retracting her thoughts from moments prior. She couldn't help herself, though.

"I will. What's up?"

When he grabbed her hand, Torin laughed and wiggled out of his embrace.

"Later. Go catch up while I relax."

Synovi handed her his debit card and cut the truck off. "A'ight. Let's go."

Another minute in the air-conditioned ride and later would turn into right now. The short stroll to the entrance of Moo's shop gave him just enough time to take in her womanly curves in the cream cotton sundress she was wearing. The color was stunning against her tanned, brown skin. Synovi shook his head with pure lust, watching her ass jiggle. Its shape symbolized the moniker he'd given her one hundred percent.

"You gon' come in and speak?" Torin asked before he could pull the door open.

Synovi frowned. "Hell no. You know I don't like people like that."

Torin snorted. "Here you go. I'll tell Moo you said what's up. Gimmie a kiss."

His hand clasped around the front of her neck, pulling her to him. Synovi kissed her slow and thoughtfully, leaving Torin no choice but to have him on her brain in his absence. Breathlessly, she looked up at him.

"See you in an hour," she spoke softly, not wanting to leave him.

Torin was down bad for her man.

He pecked her lips again for good measure and squeezed her ass. "An hour. Be good."

Synovi was forever bossing her around. Torin told him she would and entered the shop. She was grateful for days like these when they could spend time together. As busy as their schedules were, the couple still made time for one another. Pivoting, Synovi headed three doors down to a pizza spot where he was meeting Ms. Reid. Still having her in his life proved that there were truly some good human beings in this world.

He knew he could go to Torin with his feelings, but Synovi never wanted to dump too much on her. She was his girlfriend, not a therapist. Thankfully, Ms. Reid didn't mind meeting with him. In fact, she looked forward to their monthly luncheons, catching up on all his happenings. If he ever had any doubt that she didn't, the huge smile on her face proved otherwise. It matched the round belly she was toting.

"You in here stuffing your face without me," Synovi joked as she stood from the table. "What's going on?"

Ms. Reid swatted his arm before struggling to hug him. "Hey. This little boy has me eating everything in sight."

"You 'bout ready to pop, ain't it?" Synovi asked, taking a seat in one of the black cushioned chairs.

"Yes. Just two more months, and I cannot wait. I

didn't even get to enjoy the perks of being engaged before I was knocked up." Ms. Reid fake pouted.

Synovi chuckled. "Aye. Keith knew what he was doing. Lock that shit down on all levels."

Ms. Reid playfully rolled her eyes. "Mhm. I was bamboozled."

Keith, Ms. Reid's fiancé, proposed last November, and they found out she was with child in December. She'd gotten to enjoy their engagement just fine, according to Synovi. Though she and Keith were some years older than Synovi and Torin, the couple went on a few double dates together. They'd attended her baby shower, which Torin catered, and had even hired SBCS for certain jobs. Ms. Reid tried not to blur the lines between her professional role in his life and the big sisterly role she took on, but it was hard not to. In her eyes, Synovi was still the little brother she wanted to keep seeing win in life.

"That ring sitting nice, though," Synovi acknowledged, eyeing the sparkling rock on her finger.

Ms. Reid lifted her hand in the air. "Oh. You mean this ring." She blushed, wiggling her fingers. "Why, thank you. My man got it for me."

Synovi shook his head. "I'm not bouta play with you, Ms. Reid."

"I don't know how many times I have to tell you to call me Candace."

Using her professional name for so long, Synovi didn't feel right using her first name. This wasn't the first time she reminded him, and more than likely wouldn't be the last.

"It's a respect thing. What kind of pizza is this?" he questioned.

"Barbecue chicken with onions. Grab you a slice and tell me what's been going on. Congratulations again on making it to the finals."

Doing just that, Synovi snagged him a plate and placed two slices on it.

"Thank you. That shit surprised me for real."

"Really? Why? The business has grown so much."

He finished chewing and cleared his throat. "It has. I guess I'm still getting used to people coming through for me. Strangers, at that."

"Understandable. One thing you have to know is that word of mouth works. Your biggest supporters will be strangers before people you know. I see it as perfect timing. What do you think?"

"I'ont think that. We could've gotten recognized for an award months ago, and I still would've felt the same. I'm looking at it from a personal level rather than a business one. I never needed validation for my cleaning skills or leadership mentality. That feeling of wanting to belong as a person and not just a thing still lingered. I'm good now, though."

On more than one occasion, they discussed how his trauma from childhood made him feel like he wasn't wanted or needed anywhere. Having a business that people continued to reach out to despite not knowing how good of a service he provided was unbelievable to Synovi.

"When your passion and purpose align, and you find yourself doing what you love in life, know that you're right where you need to be. Shake that codependency mentality. You are enough, okay? It's not just the business people voted for, but the person behind it. Your character and the type of man you are speaks volumes."

Reassurance.

That action, especially when not asked for, meant everything to a person whose thoughts are often scattered like leaves on a blustery day. It was offered to Synovi in the healthiest of forms, and Ms. Reid hoped that he knew it was okay to receive and accept it.

"I 'preciate that. Torin said the same thing. Y'all must've been talking," Synovi joked.

She snickered. "We haven't. We just know what we're talking about. Speaking of Torin, how is she?"

My Love, he thought with the biggest smile on his face. It made Ms. Reid grin as well.

"Working her ass off. She a couple of doors down, getting her nails and toes done."

"That's exactly where I'm going when I leave here. How are you guys? Relationship still going strong?"

Synovi nodded, finishing off his second slice. "Yeah. I don't have any complaints for real. That's my baby. A nigga just trying to be the best version of himself for her, feel me? She deserves that."

Ms. Reid's heart melted at his declaration. There was so much sincerity in his words and in his eyes.

"I do. You deserve that version of yourself as well. We're human, so we evolve daily. Life happens fast, too. Our best selves are the ones being tested the most," she expressed.

Synovi knew that all too well. "For sure."

"I want you to do something for me before the next time we meet," she hinted.

"What's up?"

"Focus on not speaking or thinking negatively about yourself or the circumstances that got you to where you are today."

Synovi's mouth twitched, and his forehead creased. She was asking something of him that he almost had no control over. Subtle reminders like witnessing a father stop and tie his son's shoestrings before entering the gas station this morning made him think of how he'd never experienced that. Or how listening to GiGi cheerfully tell him about her and Torin's outings instead of it being his mama.

Circumstances were a mothafucka.

Unique's specifically.

Synovi wasn't upset about Unique handling business when it came to defending him and seeking vengeance for what Omar did to her; it was everything else before that. As much as he needed a father in his life, he needed his mother as well. It was a struggle *not* to think about those things when they'd shaped him into the man he is today. He was grateful nonetheless, though.

"I see that look on your face," Ms. Reid said. "I said to *not* think about them in a negative manner."

Flicking at his nose, Synovi let her words marinate. "I heard you. You giving me assignments, now?"

The humor in his tone made Ms. Reid chuckle.

"I always do; you're just catching on?"

Whether she came right out and told him what she thought he should work on or not, Synovi always left feeling like their time was well spent. Like he could see himself transforming by the day. That meant she was doing her job. He'd learned so much about himself and how to heal in his own way, but the journey was everlasting. You didn't stop healing because you reached new heights; you learned other ways to heal, which was instrumental to the process.

"Nah. I peeped game a minute ago. Guess you know what you doing," he jested.

"Yeah, yeah. How're things going with your mom's case?"

Synovi sighed and sat back in his seat. "She pled guilty."

Her heart sank. "Oh, no."

"Yeah. Voluntary manslaughter. She might not have to serve the entire five years, but we'll see."

Synovi saw those charges coming the minute she went to jail. Even with Rianne, Torin's lawyer she hired, on the case, she stood no chance with all the evidence against her. It was way too substantial, and Unique didn't want to put anyone through the heartache of going through a trial. Not just anyone, but Synovi specifically. She didn't want him to endure more than she'd already caused.

"She has no criminal record, right?" Ms. Reid questioned.

"Nah, she doesn't."

"Well, that's good. Maybe she can get out early on good behavior. I'll keep her in my prayers."

Synovi's head bobbed upward. "She'll appreciate that."

Their lunch meeting carried on for another fifteen minutes before they headed out and up the sidewalk to Moo's shop. Upon entering, they spotted Torin at the counter, chatting it up with another client. Synovi stood idly by, simply giving a head nod when Moo spotted him. He would've gone to sit in the car but was working on being more social. Plus, not speaking would've been rude, considering Moo was a client of his.

"There goes your boo," Moo said, tapping Torin on the arm.

Turning her head in his direction, Torin smirked. "Mean mugging and all."

"Oh, I didn't know that was your boyfriend," Loriana, the woman Torin had been talking to, said.

"Yes. You know him?"

Loriana and Moo chuckled. The way Torin's voice raised an octave humored them. It wasn't her intention for it to come off as if no one could know him. She was just curious as to how.

"Not at all. When you mentioned him having a cleaning business, I expected to see someone a bit older," Loriana answered. "That's super inspiring."

Torin smiled. Everyone always did. "Thank you."

"Of course. Be waiting for a call or an email from me. I want to connect you with a few people. Specifically, me and my husband." Loriana giggled.

"My cousin has a name." Moo snickered.

"He does, and you, like everyone else, can use it. Those rules don't apply to me," Loriana stated, making Torin chuckle.

“I heard that. Let me get on out of here. It was nice meeting you.”

Loriana beamed. “You too!”

“I’ll see you in a few weeks, Moo,” Torin said as they hugged.

“Okay, girl. Enjoy your day.”

Walking over to the duo, Ms. Reid’s belly greeted Torin first.

“Hey, mama-to-be,” she spoke.

“Hi.” Ms. Reid grinned as they hugged. “How are you?”

It was in her nature to do a wellness check.

“I’m good. How’s baby boy treating you?”

Ms. Reid chuckled. “Like he has no room in there, but other than that, he’s been showing me nothing but love.”

“That’s so good to hear. I was just telling Novi earlier this week that he’s going to sneak up on you and come early.”

She rubbed her stomach. “We’ll see. What’re y’all about to get into?”

Torin glanced Synovi’s way, wondering the same thing.

“Who knows? We’re both off today, so I’m sure we’ll get into something,” Torin answered.

“Ah. The perks of running your own business.” Ms. Reid grinned. “I’m super proud to know y’all. Congrats on your nomination, too. I saw it and was like, okay! I know that’s right. We put our votes in.”

“Thank you. I appreciate that so much.”

“Of course, girl. The way you came through in the

clutch, fixing my ridiculous cravings during this pregnancy, almost made me ask if you could move in."

The woman laughed but stopped when Synovi cleared his throat.

"Wasn't gon' be none of that," he spoke.

Humored, they shook their heads. Torin laced her fingers through his.

"Oh, hush. Wasn't anyone trying to steal her from you," Ms. Reid fussed.

"You couldn't anyway." Synovi smirked. "You ready?"

"Mhm. See you later, Candace. Text me if you need anything," Torin let her know.

Ms. Reid more than likely wouldn't, but it was the thought that counted. Synovi handed Torin a to-go container filled with pizza and boneless buffalo wings when they got in the truck. The boneless style wasn't usually her choice, but he knew she didn't like eating anything that could stain her nails right after she got them done.

"Whew. Thank you. I was in there starving," she said, taking a huge bite of the pizza as he pulled out of the parking lot.

"I told you to eat something before we left."

"You really think you're the boss of me." She laughed through chews.

Synovi glanced her way. "I'm not?"

"Nooo," she dragged, making him smirk. "You're so serious, too. That's what's funny."

He shrugged. "You stay laughing at a nigga."

"I laugh at and with you. Nothing wrong with that," she expressed.

"Nah, it ain't. If you couldn't, I'd think something was wrong. Like I don't make you happy or something. I know that ain't the case."

Torin couldn't hide the blush on her face if she wanted to. "It's not, baby. Trust me. How'd it go with Candace?"

She caught this motion of his nose twitching and knew whatever they'd discussed had triggered some emotions.

"It was coo'. Let me see your nails."

His eager calmness to shift the direction of their conversation made Torin's heartache. It wasn't that he didn't want to share with her; Synovi was just ready to move on with the day and not dwell on the past. He and Ms. Reid's conversation was considered just that. Honoring his request, Torin held her hand out.

"You like them?" she asked.

"Yeah. I can't wait to see them toes later on."

Torin snickered. "I bet you can't."

"What we on for the day? It's nice out."

"It is. I did need to run a few errands for the kitchen, but it can wait," Torin insisted.

She hardly ever got any days to herself, and even if she did, she was still trying to work. Ever since she'd gotten sick last year, Torin made sure to take her off days seriously. Plus, the Fourth of July had just passed, and she was still recouping from the holiday orders.

"A'ight. Let's slide to the Plaza and shop. I wanna cop these shoes I saw online the other day."

The outdoor shopping center was perfect to partake in today. Synovi was a simple man. He didn't splurge now that he had some money in his pocket, but he loved a fresh pair of kicks. If anything, he was buying something for Torin before himself. It felt damn good to do so, too.

"Okay. We can do that. I need to stop at Tiffany's to get another bottle of perfume."

Synovi nodded and headed toward the city. Traffic was light for a Thursday afternoon, making their drive seem much shorter. As soon as he backed into a parking spot on the first level of one of the garages, his business phone rang. It wasn't uncommon for unknown numbers to hit his line. There was something about this call that felt off, though. Synovi sensed it the second he answered.

"Hello?"

"Hi! May I speak with Mr. Black, please?" a chipper woman on the other end requested.

"This is he."

Her sigh of relief piqued Torin's interest, making her lock her phone and glance his way.

"Oh, good. This is Mrs. Lackey, the administrator at Ridgewood summer camp."

"Okay. How can I help you?" he questioned with hesitance.

"We couldn't get ahold of the girls' auntie, and you're on their list as an emergency contact."

Synovi's brows dipped. "I think you have the wrong number."

"This is Synovi Black, correct?" Mrs. Lackey quizzed.

"Yeah, but I'm not down as an emergency contact for anyone. You sure this isn't a business inquiry?"

"I'm afraid not. Mrs. Lewis has you down as her

daughter's emergency contact. Summer camp ended almost an hour ago, and the girls haven't been picked up yet."

Torin sat completely up in her seat.

"I'm sorry. You said whose daughters?" Synovi probed.

"Mrs. Lewis. Jade Lewis. Are you not Skylar and Kalie's older brother?"

Her question knocked the wind out of him. Bereft of words, Synovi stared at the dashboard screen in disbelief. This had to be some type of cruel joke.

"Hello?" Mrs. Lackey greeted.

"Yes, we're here," Torin answered, taking over the call. "What's the address to the summer camp? We'll be there as soon as we can."

Mrs. Lackey rattled off the address while Torin typed it into Google Maps on her phone.

"See you shortly," Mrs. Lackey said, hanging up.

Torin blinked once, twice, and a third time before she found the words to speak. "I don't even know what to say right now."

Synovi's jaw clenched, mimicking the motion of his hand gripping the steering wheel. "Jade don' lost her fucking mind," he hissed, pulling out of the parking garage.

Gulping, Torin nodded. She couldn't agree more.

four

Healing was so damn frustrating.

One minute, Synovi was proud of himself for doing well, forgiving himself and others for the past, and learning to process the pain, and in an instant, more traumatic situations arose. He couldn't shake the drama if his life depended on it. That phone call from Mrs. Lackey made him feel like all his progress had been done in vain.

"Do you want me to come in with you?" Torin asked as they pulled up to the building.

Synovi shook his head no. He hadn't uttered a word on the drive over, but his anger was felt. It radiated off him in waves, making Torin want to crank the air up more.

"Okay," she mumbled softly, sinking further into her seat.

Hitting the locks, Synovi climbed out and headed toward the entrance. Torin didn't understand Jade's motives. It'd been almost a year since they ran into her at the grocery store, and they hadn't heard a peep out of her since. The audacity of her to maliciously add Synovi to her daughter's emergency contact list was vile. Fucking disgusting and reckless, to say the least.

"I really can't believe this." Torin huffed, watching the doors of the school.

She'd kept her cool the entire ride, not wanting to rile Synovi up even more, but when the time presented itself, Torin would make sure Jade received the tongue-lashing she should've given her long before now.

When Synovi entered the office he'd been escorted to after checking in, his temper simmered immediately. The two little girls sitting before him didn't deserve to feel those emotions when they'd done nothing wrong. His stomach churned when Mrs. Lackey acknowledged him.

"Ah, you made it," she said, standing from her chair. "I'm Mrs. Lackey. Nice to meet you."

The Black woman looked to be in her midforties and had a pleasant smile.

He shook her outstretched hand. "Synovi."

Skylar, the oldest of the two girls, was the first to greet him. "You're our brother."

For a second time today, Synovi had gotten the wind knocked out of him. Skylar spoke the words with so much confidence that if he wasn't their brother, she'd made Synovi a believer.

"Y-Yeah," he mumbled.

He didn't have many words to say but knew he had to locate them.

"Sorry if coming to get them inconvenienced you," Mrs. Lackey said.

"Nah. It was no problem at all."

That was a lie, but he'd never admit it aloud. Especially in their presence.

"You girls ready to go?" Mrs. Lackey asked.

"Yes!" Skylar cheered, hopping up from her seat.

Beside her, Kalie slowly climbed down from the chair. She hadn't spoken a word but had been staring a hole into Synovi the entire time.

Ain't no telling what the fuck their mama don' told them about me, Synovi thought.

"Come on, Kalie. We're going with Brother," Skylar said, helping her put her cheetah print backpack on.

Kalie looked up at him and gave a shy smile.

"What's up, baby girl?" he said with ease, surprising himself.

Those words must've surprised Skylar, too, because she gasped. "How'd you know that was her nickname?"

Her excitement made him smirk. "Lucky guess."

"Hi," Kalie spoke softly.

Mrs. Lackey chuckled with amazement. "She must be fond of you. We can hardly get her to say two words to us."

"Really?" Synovi questioned.

He found that odd but then considered all they'd probably gone through, and it hit him. Traumatic experiences made him not like speaking either. There wasn't much to talk about with people you didn't trust, so he didn't. Synovi couldn't help but wonder what Kalie's young, innocent eyes and ears had been privy to. The thought sickened him.

"Yes," Mrs. Lackey answered as they walked out of

the office. "She hasn't always been like that, though. It didn't start until their father was killed."

She whispered the last sentence, and bile bubbled in Synovi's throat. He knew there was no way she knew he, in some way, was the reason for Kalie's sudden mutism. And if she did know, Mrs. Lackey didn't show it. The news article and video of Omar's killing had been shared on so many platforms that Synovi knew the school had to have been vetted on how to handle Skylar and Kalie moving forward.

Jade's audacity was at an all-time high. Synovi didn't know if this was her way of trying to get back at him, but he was checking her ass as soon as he saw her.

"Damn," was all Synovi mumbled as they made it outside.

"Is that your truck?" Skylar questioned, facing him.

Synovi bobbed his head. "Yeah."

"Oooh," she cooed, racing toward it with Kalie's hand grasped in hers.

"Aye!" Synovi called out, halting Skylar's footsteps immediately.

She faced him with wide eyes as if she'd never had someone yell at her before. Synovi immediately felt like shit.

He lowered his tone. "Don't run off, a'ight? Wait for me right there, and we'll walk together." He pointed to a spot away from the curb.

Skylar took one small step in that direction and smirked. "Here?"

"Walk some more," Synovi instructed.

Like she was creeping, Skylar landed in the spot he'd told her to and smiled. "There. Now, we wait."

Synovi was already stressed, and they hadn't even left the premises. Skylar was going to give him a run for his money for sure. He sighed and faced Mrs. Lackey, who grinned.

"Ms. Skylar is a handful, but she's the sweetest. A little sneaky, but what child isn't?"

"Right. Is this the first time she hasn't come to pick them up?" Synovi asked.

It was Mrs. Lackey's turn to sigh. "Unfortunately, not. You guys's Aunt Simone normally picks them up, but it looks like she was removed from the emergency contact list a week ago."

Her insinuating that Simone was his auntie let Synovi know everything he needed to know regarding her knowledge of the situation.

"I wasn't aware of that," he said.

"Yeah. We've had multiple talks with Jade about being on time to get them, but I'm guessing it goes in one ear and out the other. I try my best to advocate for them, knowing what they've been through, but someone else might not be as accommodating. It's summer camp, so our hours and duties aren't as tedious, but her tardiness cannot happen during the normal school year anymore. CPS will be contacted if so."

Those three letters put a sour taste in Synovi's mouth.

Mrs. Lackey didn't come off like the social workers or teachers he encountered as a kid; she was just a woman doing her job and looking out for her students. It was heartwarming until it wasn't, which would happen if Jade didn't get her shit together.

"I'll have a talk with her. Thanks for calling me," Synovi said.

"No problem. Thank you for moving quickly. Girls! See you tomorrow." She waved, and they did the same.

Exhaling, Synovi pivoted and walked toward them. He eyed their drastically different outfits and hairstyles. Skylar had on leggings, a Barbie graphic tee, low, pink Dunks, and her hair was in a braided ponytail with a bow. Wanting to match her sister's shoe color but not her outfit, Kalie had on sparkling pink cowboy boots, a multicolored tutu skirt, and a white long-sleeved shirt with a purple denim jacket vest over it. Her hair was styled in two big afro puffs, with baby hairs framing her forehead.

She was in that stage of dressing herself, and Synovi could tell. The outfit screamed personality, and he fucked with that, seeing how she wasn't much of a talker. She expressed herself through her wardrobe.

"Can we move now?" Skylar questioned, adjusting her metallic hot pink backpack.

Synovi shook his head at her smart-aleck question. "Yeah. Come on."

She took ahold of Kalie's hand, and they skipped toward the truck. Inside it, Torin told herself to calm down and act like her nerves weren't getting the best of her. Synovi opened the backdoor for them to climb inside. Skylar did so by herself, and he helped Kalie into the seat.

Crossing one leg over the other, she stared up at him.

Synovi felt like he was staring down at a younger girl version of himself. Kalie's eyes were mysteriously dark and beautiful as black satin. She rubbed at them, indicating it was almost that time of day for a nap.

"You sleepy?" He couldn't help but ask.

Kalie just smiled softly.

"She is!" Skylar belted. "She didn't get much sleep last night. Hi! What's your name?" she asked Torin, who was already facing them.

Synovi assumed Kalie knew how to put her seatbelt on herself, but when she didn't reach for it, he did the honors. Closing her door, he walked to the driver's side and glanced at the sky.

"Yo, my man. I don't know what you're on, but help a nigga out. Please." He sighed before climbing inside.

"My name is Torin. What's your name?"

Skylar smirked. "Skylar. This is Kalie," she said, pointing to her sister.

"Hi, Kalie." Torin waved. "I love your hair."

She simply smiled before yawning.

"You like my hair, too? My auntie friend did it," Skylar interjected.

"I do like it. Ours is similar."

Moving her braids to the front of her, Torin let Skylar examine them. That seemed like something she was interested in doing, and she was right.

"They're so long! I want mine to be that long, but my mama said I'm not old enough yet."

Pouting, she huffed and pressed herself against the seat. Torin glanced at Synovi, who hadn't made an attempt to pull out of the parking lot yet. Rubbing his arm, Torin garnered his attention.

“Everything’s gonna be okay.”

The conviction in her statement wasn’t as strong as Synovi needed it to be. He heard her, though, and wanted to believe everything would be okay.

“Are you taking us home?” Skylar questioned, leaning on the middle console between them.

It didn’t hit him until now that he didn’t know where they lived. Noticing the frustration on his face, Torin took over.

“Yes. Can you tell me your address so I can put it in the GPS?”

Skylar rattled off their address, and Torin typed it in. As much as he would’ve liked complete silence on the nineteen-minute ride, Synovi was grateful Torin turned on some music. She was trying to make everyone as comfortable as possible. The tunes masked their anxiousness while Skylar sang along with them. Peeking over her shoulder, she spotted Kalie already knocked out.

Grabbing Synovi’s hand, Torin kissed the back of it. She held onto it until they pulled into their driveway. The home was a vast difference from the one Synovi had visited more than he should’ve.

Parking, he stared at the townhome with disgust and rattled nerves. *How the fuck did we get to this point*? He thought. Answers he knew he wouldn’t get bothered Synovi the most. The eerily disturbing thoughts he had about harming Jade hadn’t fled his mind on the ride over, and he hated it. That wasn’t the type of person he was.

Synovi's days of harming someone who'd inflicted pain on him had passed long ago. The treatment he gave Unique before knowing her situation was replaced with grace. Jade didn't deserve an ounce of that. After all she'd taken him through, this was the stunt she wanted to pull. Synovi was pissed off but had to show some type of restraint, or he'd end up behind bars.

"I should've had them call to see if she's here," he mumbled lowly but loud enough for Skylar to hear.

"She's probably sleeping," she announced.

Synovi glanced at the time on the dash. It was the middle of the afternoon. There was no way her ass should've been catching z's while her kids were abandoned. That angered him even more, and before he let more thoughts fester, he unfastened his seatbelt and pushed the door open.

"Come on," he told Skylar. She went to wake Kalie up, but he stopped her. "I'll grab your sister."

"Okay. See you later... What's your name again?" she asked.

Torin smiled. "It's Torin."

Giggling, Skylar said, "Right! See you later, Torin."

With a wave, she hopped out of the truck, clutching her backpack in her hand. Kalie stayed fast asleep as Synovi lifted her into his arms and grabbed her belongings. Closing the door, he stepped to Torin's door, and she lowered the window.

"I'll be right back," he declared.

"I'll be right here."

Her words held more meaning than the moment they shared.

It'd been at least a minute of them standing at the door, waiting for Jade to open it. Synovi's patience was non-existent. Adjusting Kalie in his arms, she snuggled closer to him as he pressed the doorbell again. Skylar followed behind him, incessantly pushing the silver button.

"We gotta press it a bunch of times, sometimes," she informed.

He wanted to ask what they did when she didn't come to the door, but the sound of the locks turning stopped him. Synovi inhaled and gritted his teeth as he came face to face with his past. Jade was a mess. Not just mentally, which he'd long ago learned, but physically as well.

The dried slobber on her face was evidence that she'd been knocked out. A baggy, stained t-shirt draped her while her hair sat tangled in a bun at the top of her head. The stench emitting from her body made Synovi frown. It deepened when she finally opened her mouth to speak. Jade was either drunk or hungover.

"You guys made it home." She grinned lazily.

"Our brother came to get us," Skylar said. "Thank goodness."

The relief in her voice caused Synovi to clench his jaw. She, too, was fed up with her mother's antics.

"Uh. Don't say it like that. He should've been picking y'all up anyway," Jade slurred.

"Okay, Mama. Here. I'll carry Kalie inside, so you don't have to come in," Skylar offered.

Synovi was glad she did because he had no plans to step inside their house unless necessary. At five years old,

Kalie was a little ol' thing compared to Skylar's ten-year-old tall, lanky stature. He handed her over and swallowed the lump in his throat.

"Will we see you again?" Skylar questioned with bright eyes.

The hopefulness in her tone tightened his chest.

"I'm not sure yet, but be good, a'ight?"

Her mood dampened as she mumbled, "Okay."

Thankfully, Skylar disappeared inside the house, away from the door. Synovi didn't need her to hear what he was about to say. The smirk Jade had plastered on her face was wiped smooth off.

"Bitch, have you lost your mind?" Synovi hissed, stepping up to her. "Why would you put me down as their emergency contact, and you know I want nothing to do with your ass?"

Jade crossed her arms. "They're your sisters. I shouldn't have to ask you to do a damn thing! Their father isn't here, so someone has to step up to the plate."

Synovi pinched the bridge of his nose. His blood simmered hearing those words and her reasoning. It was a pathetic one, but he was in no mood to hear any more from her.

"They're not my responsibility." His voice was low, words firm. Synovi needed her to understand the severity of his words.

"Oh, they're not? Isn't that what *big brothers* are for? Picking up the slack when the parent falls off. I mean, damn. They have a right to know who you really are."

"For what? You just want to start more mess, and I ain't going for it."

Her lips pursed outward. "Why not? It's not my fault Sky saw a picture of you in my phone and asked questions. Was I supposed to lie to her?"

"Like lying is something new for you." Synovi scoffed. "Take me off that list, Jade."

"No can do. I'm depressed and need help. Thanks to you and your deranged ass mama, their daddy was killed. Why should they suffer, too?"

Synovi clenched his fist and chuckled angrily. "You know what... I'ma walk off before I hurt you."

Without hesitation, he pivoted and took two steps down the sidewalk. If he didn't remove himself from the situation, it was going to get ugly quickly. Before he could get any further, Jade pounded her fist into his back before yanking on his t-shirt.

"Don't walk away from me!" she shouted.

Losing his cool, Synovi jerked around and roughly clasped a hand around her neck. Jade's body slammed into the front door with a thud. Torin had been nervously waiting in the car, not wanting to stir the pot any more than it already was, but she was out of it the second Jade's fingers grasped his shirt.

"Novi!" Torin yelled, running up the sidewalk.

All he saw was red as his hold tightened. He wanted to choke the life out of her. End hers how she tried to ruin his. Jade wasn't remorseful at all. It showed in the glimmer of her eyes as she stared up at him. This was what she wanted. She intentionally added his name and business number to their emergency contact list in hopes that she'd get his attention.

"Synovi, let her go," Torin pleaded, grabbing his arm.

It was no use. Synovi's anger and strength were no match right now.

"Baby, please. Don't let her take you to that dark place. She's not worth it."

His hand tightened at her statement, and he gritted his teeth.

"I'ma tell you this one time, so listen to me carefully. Leave me the fuck out of your life. Forget I ever existed and act like you never knew me."

Synovi released her, and Jade inhaled harshly. She sucked in deep breaths but didn't seem to care about her oxygen levels once she noticed Torin struggling to pull Synovi away.

"Y-You had m-my kids around this bitch!" Jade spat, walking up to Torin.

With enough force to make her reconsider her actions, Torin mushed her in the face with her full palm, making Jade fall hard on her ass.

"If you don't back the fuck up," Torin hissed.

She tried to let Synovi handle the situation, but it was game over when Jade put her hands on him. Scrambling to her feet, Jade tugged her shorts back into place.

"Run up on me again, and I'ma make sure you get a spot right next to your husband," Torin said eerily calm.

"Fuck you! You show up with him dropping my kids off!" she screamed, patting her chest. "You're the reason everything is fucked up now. You should've just let us be together!"

Synovi shook his head as Torin snapped.

"Let y'all be together? Do you hear how sick you sound? You need to learn accountability, with your delusional ass. Focus on raising your daughters and putting the bottle down!" Torin shouted, pointing a finger her way and walking up on her.

It was Synovi's turn to pull her back.

"C'mon, Love. We're wasting our breath."

"Don't worry about my kids, hoe! We're good. Just know he is going to always be in their life, whether you like it or not." Jade laughed. "Focus on that!"

She walked off toward the house, slamming the door after entering. Synovi and Torin walked briskly to the truck and hopped inside before skirting out of the driveway. Their adrenaline was on ten, and their minds were all over the place.

"I can't believe her," Torin fussed. "She had the nerve to put her hands on you and talk crazy like that. Oooh. She's lucky I was trying to keep it cool for you."

Her leg bounced, and her nostrils flared as Synovi came to a stop sign. His silence was suffocating until it wasn't. Torin glanced over at him. His chest heaved, trying to find the words to say. Only one came to mind.

"Love," he called out.

Torin leaned over the console, wrapping him in an embrace that made tears prick her eyes. His hands were trembling. "I can't let her fuck up my peace. I can't."

Pulling his head into her chest, she soothingly massaged the back of his head and neck. "I won't let her. We won't let her. Okay?"

Synovi couldn't acknowledge her words. Not even with a nod. Deep down, he knew this was only the beginning of Jade's bullshit, and Torin hoped she'd be able to keep her promise.

five

A girls's night was exactly what Torin needed after the day she had.

A dollop of wine remained in the espresso brown wine glass, and next to it sat a shot of tequila. It was one of those kinds of nights.

"You've been babysitting that shot for way too long, girl," Leighton examined.

Torin sucked her teeth, reclaiming her spot on the sectional. "I had to use the bathroom and get myself together."

Whenever she drank wine, it wasn't the kind you needed multiple glasses of to feel. And right now, she didn't want to feel anything. One glass of Money Mango by Geselle Wine had her buzzing. Her cellar inside the pantry stayed stocked with her favorites from the Black-owned brand.

"Mhm. Get yourself even more together and toss that shot back, miss ma'am," Mia, Torin's assistant and friend, said.

"Y'all need to take one, too," Torin urged. "I'm not about to be the only drunk one."

"We already have ours ready!" Leighton laughed.

She eyed their glasses and smirked. "Oh. Okay, then."

They giggled and clinked glasses before tapping the table and throwing them back. Torin didn't even frown as the warm liquid settled in her chest.

"Whew," Mia expressed. "That's my last one."

"Mine too, before we be pulling up on a bitch and mushing her head in again."

Torin said the words so casually that Leighton and Mia's laughs startled her.

"What?" Torin questioned. "I'm so serious. Y'all just don't know how bad I wanted to whoop her ass."

"What stopped you?" Mia questioned.

"For one, the kids were there. I was trying to have some type of decorum, but that hoe put her nasty hands on my man." Torin scoffed.

"You better than me." Leighton sighed. "I'm proud of you, though. I would've bailed you out of jail."

"Because that's exactly where I would've been going. She seems like the police type of hoe," Torin said.

Mia nodded. "Mhm. Have y'all heard from her since?"

It'd been over a week since they dropped the girls off at home, and Jade hadn't let up since. The constant calls to Synovi's business phone were ignored, and she'd even gone as far as emailing the SBCS email account. Thankfully, she hadn't popped up because a restraining order was next up. Torin was peeved, to say the least.

"Yes, and I keep telling him something is mentally

wrong with her. It's like she's obsessed." Torin huffed with frustration.

"She's basically like, if I can't have the daddy anymore, might as well try to get with the son again." Leighton laughed.

"Bitch," Torin sputtered. "Shut up. She's deranged. Then had the nerve to have Skylar, the oldest daughter, leave Synovi a voice note from her iPad."

The friends gasped.

"You lying," Mia whispered. "What'd it say?"

"That she wants to see him again and hoped he and her mama can get along."

Leighton blew out a breath. "That's... intense."

"Beyond," Mia chimed. "She's how old?"

"Ten. So, I don't know if she made her send that or if Skylar sent it on her own."

They were laid up in bed earlier that week when the message came through from an email address. The depths Jade had gone through to try and get his attention were extreme, so they didn't put it past her to have Skylar doing the same.

"Eh, that's questionable. These kids are geniuses with technology. My niece sends me voice notes all the time, and she's six," Mia voiced.

"True. Either way, the fact that *that's* the message she sent lets me know Jade is over there talking crazy about us. You can't convince me otherwise."

The ladies nodded, completely agreeing.

"Let's pray that she's not," Mia said. "How are you really feeling, though? I know this is a lot to handle."

Torin tilted her head, and her eyes began to water.

"Awww, friend," Leighton cooed.

Sniffling, Torin cleared her throat. "Y'all not hot?"

The trio giggled, knowing that meant she was drunk.

"Seriously, though... I'm sad for Synovi and those girls. It's heartbreaking watching him battle with his emotions on what to do. The good person in him wants to do more, but he knows the consequences it'll come with."

"And then their school situation," Mia added. "That's more concerning than anything."

"Right. The entire situation is triggering, and honestly, I don't see anything good coming from it."

She hated to say that, but Torin was being realistic with herself. A person like Jade stopped at nothing until she got what she wanted. She waited months to pull her stunts, and Torin hoped like hell this one didn't end in tragedy. There was only so much she was willing to put up with, especially from a hating ass hoe who liked to fuck on their dead husband's son. She still couldn't believe that.

"Well, we're gonna stay positive. Try to, at least." Mia giggled before yawning.

"Those drinks snuck up on you, huh?" Leighton teased.

Mia grabbed her water bottle, twisted the cap, and guzzled some down. "Yes. You hoes have me turning up on a weekday."

"Thankfully, tomorrow's schedule is light," Torin noted. "We only have three jobs."

That was heaven to Mia's ears. Some days, they were on the go from sun up to sun down. With it being the summer and so many events being hosted, Kaine's Kitchen calendar was jam-packed. She wouldn't trade being Torin's assistant for anything, though. The way she soaked up knowledge from her and been put on so many gems would come in handy in the long run whenever she decided to branch off and start her own consulting business.

"That's the best news I've heard all week." Mia laughed. "Speaking of news. What're you wearing to the awards show?"

"Right, because you haven't mentioned two things about it," Leighton probed.

"My mind has been all over the place. I'll start looking this weekend."

The KCPCA was the type of event where you put that shit on. Torin studied some of the pictures from the previous award shows and knew right away that she'd want to wear a long silk gown, an up-do type of hairstyle, and match Synovi.

"No, you need to start looking tonight. The show is in two weeks, girl," Leighton fussed.

"Ugh. Not tonight. I'll go by MAG Co. tomorrow and see what they have."

Mia snapped her fingers. "They did just drop their elegant gown collection. I'll meet you there."

"We can ride together. There's a two-hour break between our second and last job," Torin said.

"Glad I didn't want to come," Leighton fake fussed, standing from the couch. "I have hair to do anyway."

Torin giggled. "Girl, please. Like I wasn't going to FaceTime you so you could be there anyway."

"Mhm. You a real one, so I know you was. Want me to put this food up?" Leighton questioned, heading toward the kitchen.

Torin had prepared some presto chicken flatbread with wings for dinner. It was something quick but hearty and delicious.

"No, I got it. I'ma warm Novi up some when he gets here."

"Baby, what I wouldn't give to come home to your cooking every night," Mia said, gathering the glasses from the table.

"Please. Like you can't cook."

"That's the point." Mia laughed. "I don't want to damn near every day."

"Then she got a man who cleans up behind her, too!" Leighton shouted.

Mia looked down at the glasses in her hand before setting them right back on the table. "She sure does. Let me leave these here for him."

Torin laughed loudly. "Don't make me hurt you. He doesn't *always* clean up behind me."

"It's the loving fact that he does and is good at it. What was that prayer again?"

"Which one? There were a bunch." Torin laughed but was serious.

After her breakup with Don, she focused on her business and put one hundred percent of herself into Kaine's Kitchen. She hadn't been looking for a man but had to admit that she did get lonely. Synovi, in all his rude sexiness, made his presence known in her home, heart, and head and hadn't vacated since. Not only had she prayed for a man who valued her, but one who helped take more than a few loads off her shoulders.

Synovi had done just that. He'd also added a few stressors in there, but Torin didn't dwell on those. Life wasn't perfect. It was far from it, but they made it work for them. All the good with them outweighed the bad, and for that, she was grateful and would continue praying over their union. Worship didn't stop because she received what she'd asked Him for.

Fifteen minutes later, the girls were headed home. Torin bid them a good night and washed the few dishes in the sink, plus their glasses, and wiped the counters down before heading upstairs. The amount of yawning she did in less than ten minutes was sad and proof that the liquor was on her ass. Once she reached her bedroom, she crawled into bed and unlocked her phone to text Synovi.

She missed him, and he hadn't gone anywhere.

Not physically, anyway.

Mentally, Synovi was struggling to stay above water. He hated that someone who meant nothing to him had so much power over his daily thoughts. He'd tried implementing the skills Ms. Reid taught him, but thinking positively about such a negative situation while in the thick of it was maddening and damn near impossible to do.

So, he spent his days in the gym. If he wasn't at work, he was burning pent-up energy while exercising. It'd been his vice, and Torin wondered when it'd gone from her to a physical location. She thought she was home...

his safe place, yet he was straying away as if he no longer belonged. It made her sick to her stomach.

Dialing his number, she waited for him to answer the FaceTime call. Synovi answered on the third ring, with darkness surrounding him.

"What's up, Love?" he spoke. His voice was thick with emotion that made her skin tingle.

Torin licked her lips. "Hey. You're not at the gym."

It was an assessment of his background, not a question.

"Nah. I'm out front."

She hadn't heard her camera notifications go off.

"Oh, okay. You coming in?"

The uncertainty in her question had him powering his truck off and climbing out. She always said so much without saying anything, and Synovi listened. He heard her loud and clear.

"Yeah, here I come now."

Torin stayed on the phone, watching his every move as he entered her home through the garage. His hood was pulled over his head, resembling his dampened mood. Synovi toed his shoes off, placed them under the bench, and discarded his keys in the wooden bowl on the entry table. Trudging through the kitchen, he briefly glanced at the spread on the counter.

He had no appetite for food.

Only her.

Neither hung up the phone until Synovi walked up the stairs and entered her bedroom door. His yearning presence filled the desolate space instantly. Torin propped herself up on her elbow. The center of Synovi's gray joggers captured her attention. Without shame, she drank in his solid physique. He was much buffer but still soft enough to lay on, and she loved that.

"See something you like?" he challenged with a smirk.

Licking her lips, Torin nodded. "Mhm. I do."

"I see something I like, too. Something I need."

He climbed onto the bed, pulling her body atop his in a way that made Torin whimper. With ease, his arm glided between her legs, and his hand cupped her soft ass as he entangled their legs. Hers over his waist and one of his between hers. The gentle caress he gave her cheeks while simultaneously grazing her pussy with his palm made Torin's back arch. She tightened the hold she had around his neck and relaxed against him without being told to do so.

"Love," Synovi crooned.

He always spoke her name with earnest delight as if it were his obligation to remind her that's what she was. That she was all he felt when in her presence. The trail of his warm hand rubbing up and down her back made Torin shiver with need. Their skin-to-skin connection was her favorite. Synovi nestled his face in the crook of her neck and inhaled.

"Tell me something good," Synovi urged.

"You smell good."

Her smile against his neck made Synovi pull her closer to him. If he could, he'd merge their bodies together. Torin wouldn't object to that. Needy. Urgent. Clingy by default. That was how they made one another feel.

"What else? How was your day?"

She pressed her lips against his neck, peppering soft kisses while breathing in the fresh smell of him. Instead of going to the gym, he'd showered at his condo and came straight to her.

"It was fine." She hummed.

"Did you miss me?"

Torin giggled, then softly moaned as he massaged the back of her neck.

"Yes. Always."

Her response was breathy, as if she couldn't believe he asked that.

"I missed you more," he declared.

"Did you? I don't like when you go missing on me."

Her confession was made as she straddled his lap, easing her hands around his tattooed-covered neck. Squinting, she applied pressure. Synovi licked his lips.

"A'ight. Tell me what you want from me, Love. Let's make it simple. I don't ever want you to feel like this ain't where I wanna be. What do you need from me?"

The intimate moment Synovi was trying to have was overshadowed by Torin's arousal. Her nipples puckered, straining against the cotton of her tank. The liquor-induced lust in her eyes heightened.

"Right now." She breathed, grinding in his lap. "I need you to fuck me."

Synovi smirked and gripped her hips. "I'm trying to see what's going on in that pretty little head of yours, and you wanna get freaky. I don't always have to stick my dick in you."

"But I want you to," she whined in response. "I like it when you do that."

Synovi's deep chortle didn't deter his erection from making itself known. It tented his joggers, begging to be set free. Torin knew what her whimpers did to him. They broke down every barrier he tried keeping up.

"I *love* it when you take this dick, too, but right now, I need you to tell me what's wrong."

Her pout and fake petulant mood almost made him give in. Synovi planned to give her exactly what her throbbing center wanted as soon as she answered his question. She pinned her eyes on him, giving in.

"You've been distant. Not physically, but I can tell the situation with your sisters is heavy on your mind," Torin confessed.

My heart, too, Synovi thought.

"You keep telling me you're okay, but I know you're not. I know you, Novi. You don't have to hide from me. It hurts me knowing I can't do much to ease the pain and annoyance you feel."

Synovi absentmindedly caressed her thighs. "What else?"

She was assailed by confusion and pressure.

"What do you mean?"

"I asked what's wrong with you, not me. I'm not concerned about shit that I can't control right now. Still working on getting out of my head about it, though. You, on the other hand, I'ma always give a fuck about. You don't think I notice how all over the place you've been lately?"

"It's just a lot going on," Torin insisted.

"A'ight. Like what? Keeping me in the blind isn't going to help me help you take the stress away. Giving you some dick ain't either."

Her brow lifted, wanting to test that theory. Synovi went to lift her off him, and she giggled.

"Okay, okay. You know how I get trying to do a million things at once. Racquel and her dorm situation is one. I need to hire more staff. I accidentally overbooked two parties for next weekend. I'm still waiting on the approval of my spices from the FDA. I need to book all my appointments and find a dress for the awards. Just... a whole fucking lot."

Synovi cleared his throat. "Worrying about your sister and the decisions she makes, thinking she's going to fail gon' give you gray hairs. Let her come to the realization that you and your mama were right."

Torin sighed. "Okay, fine."

"Tell Mia to go through the applications and vet the people who applied. That's what she gets paid to do. I know you like to run shit your way, but you gotta leave the tasks you delegated to folks to them."

Her lip poked out, but she heard him. It was something Torin struggled with. Every entrepreneur she knew or had watched grow went through a phase of wanting to do it all. Her business was her baby, and like mothers caring for their children but never taking the time to care for themselves, Torin would soon be burnt out. Not on Synovi's watch.

She nodded, and he effortlessly continued dishing

out solutions. It was the problem solver in him. If Synovi didn't do anything else in this life, he was going to figure some shit the hell out and make it work. For his woman, he'd become the ultimate troubleshooter.

"I'll rearrange my cleanings this weekend and have Tae pick them up, so you'll have extra hands for the double booking."

"I thought he was on probation?"

"He is. This'll be his first test back in the field," he answered, scratching at his low-trimmed beard.

Torin sighed with relief. "Okay. I guess I just needed to talk it out and game plan."

"I know." Synovi smirked, running his hands underneath her tank top. "How long does it normally take to hear something back from the FDA?"

"They said a minimum of twelve months, which it hasn't been yet. I was looking for some type of update."

Expanding her brand meant so much to Torin. Creating her own spice blends to sell was one of them. She'd started the process over a year ago and was anxious to get the ball rolling. What she hadn't anticipated was the waiting process.

"I'ont know too much about regulations in culinary, but wouldn't they reach out when everything is finalized or if there was an issue?" Synovi questioned.

With her head cocked to the side and lips pursed, Torin hummed. "Yeah. That makes sense. I need to learn patience."

He chuckled. "Yeah. You do. Everything gon' fall through exactly how it's supposed to. Don't trip. Trust the process and your talent, Love."

She kissed his soft lips. "Thank you. I needed to hear those words. I'll schedule my hair and nail appointments in the morning."

"Yeah, handle that. Anything else?" Synovi yawned, rubbing on her booty.

"Nope." She chuckled. "I feel much better now. You always take care of me even when I know I'm dramatic sometimes."

"That's what I'm supposed to do. Now," he said, rolling them over. "Take these clothes off so you can stop begging."

Torin went to yelp with laughter at his bossiness, but Synovi captured it with a languid kiss. It was tender, filled with affection, and just what she needed. He was forcing her to keep her composure when she wanted to do everything but that.

"Baby," Torin cooed once he peeled her tank top and bra off.

He trailed kisses down her neck, swirled his tongue around her protruding nipples and sucked. Torin's back arched as he multi-tasked and peeled her leggings and no-show thong off. She didn't know when he'd lowered his head between her thighs, but she felt every gust of breath from him as he kissed her thighs and ran his fingers over her slit.

"Pussy soaking wet," he murmured.

Swollen and throbbing with need, Torin moaned as Synovi spread the folds of her labia and thumbed her clit. He stroked the nub at a steady pace and angled his body sideways. Placing her right leg over his shoulder, draping his defined back, he stretched the left one out. This position allowed him to please with side-to-side movement rather than up-and-down motions.

"Baby, please," Torin groaned with frustration.

"Ssshh, " Synovi hushed her. "I got you."

He kissed her clit before gently slurping it into his mouth.

And, he indeed did. The sensation of him horizontally flickering her clit made her body jerk. Every nerve ending was heightened as her orgasm quickly approached. He palmed her mound, easing her clitoral hood back. Torin choked on a gasp as he did tricks with his tongue and suctioned her bundle of nerves while sliding two fingers inside of her.

She spread her legs wider and cried his name. "Novi!"

"Mhm. I feel it," he noted, feeling her walls contract. "Give me that shit."

Her legs clamped around his head the same way his mouth did her sex. Synovi was relentless in his pursuit to make her cum. He *needed* her to relax and know that her man had her under any circumstances. She quivered around his fingers as he tapped on her G-spot.

"Oh, my gosh!" She squealed, gripping the sheets.

Synovi pressed his face deeper into her, making Torin swirl her hips. She rode the waves of pleasure as he gripped her ass, stuffing his face like she was one of her full-course meals. Her stomach hollowed, and the lower half of her body thrust upward as she came. *Hard.*

The sounds of him slurping her juices echoed throughout the room, but all Torin heard was white noise. It invaded her head like a thick fog at sunrise. Her satisfied, overwhelming moans didn't penetrate the air for more than a few seconds. When they did, she was gasping for air, and her heart thundered wildly as if she were about to pass out.

Quivering, she reached for Synovi. "Come h-here. I need to feel you."

Obliging, he lifted, removing his fingers slowly. In nothing but his briefs now, he situated himself between her legs, pushed them back, and stuck his fingers in his mouth. Torin watched, giving him a smoldering gaze. Not wanting to leave her out of the taste test, Synovi recoated his fingers with her essence before sliding them inside her and swirling. When he pulled them out again, he gave her a command she readily followed.

"Open your mouth."

Torin's jaw dropped, and her tongue snaked out. With heated eyes, Synovi slid his fingers into her mouth, and she closed her lips around them, sucking them clean. A guttural groan sounded from the back of his throat.

"Mmm. I taste good on you," Torin said.

Her eyes were low, and a content smile lifted her flushed cheekbones. Removing his briefs, Synovi stroked his dick using the mess he'd made between her legs as a lubricant. Torin squirmed, but not for long. He tapped his bulbous tip along her wetness, making a fucking mess, and smirked before sliding deep inside her. Torin whimpered as he stretched her out and leaned over to slide his tongue in her mouth.

"Fuck!" She cried, breaking their lip lock and clawing at his back. "Right there, right there!"

Synovi long stroked her, circling his hips. He wasn't going anywhere, not until he was good and ready to.

"I'm not coming up out of this pussy until I've fucked the stress up out of you," he declared, kissing her cheek. "Keep nutting on this dick, Love."

It was about to be a long night.

six

Outside of cooking, there was nothing Torin loved more than content days for Kaine's Kitchen.

Okay. She had a deep passion for a few other things, but none of them lifted her spirit quite like elevating her business. Inside an Airbnb she'd rented for the day, various food dishes in burners decorated the countertops. People bought with their eyes first, so capturing mouthwatering photos and videos was key. With food often being the pinnacle of any type of event, she wanted to make booking and hiring her an experience before the big day.

Serving a diverse set of clients, Torin ensured her photographer snapped pictures for various settings. An office luncheon, meal-prep trays, a baby shower table, and appetizers for a wedding were just a few scenes she shot. She hired models to come in at set times and compensated them for their involvement.

Since being nominated for best chef and catering services, inquiries and bookings have been pouring in.

Torin wasn't concerned with winning, even though it'd be a nice accolade to add to her résumé. She'd be a fool not to seize the opportunity to service a new audience and grow her business, though.

"I cannot wait until the website is updated," Mia said as the photographer, Erin, gave her a sneak peek from her camera.

Smiling, Torin agreed. "I know, right? Adding videos is going to take it to the next level."

It was that time of the year when she revamped her entire brand. Although her spices hadn't been approved yet, Torin still had mockups of the seasonings at the shoot. She'd been selling them to a few family members and friends since perfecting their blends over the years, but the public would have to wait. There was so much reward in being patient, and she was learning that.

"Am I getting paid for my acting skills today?" one of the models for the last shoot asked.

Torin chuckled. "Racquel, please don't start. I'm compensating you with food."

"I mean, I guess that's fine." She giggled. "I'm not too good for a free meal. Now, what am I supposed to do?"

"You can start with staying off your phone. No, actually," Torin drew back. "Stay on it. Whoever you've been texting has you grinning like crazy."

Rosiness tinted Racquel's cheeks even more. She hated when her sister, anyone really, called her out.

"Awww. Look at her," Mia teased. "Lil' baby has a crush on somebody."

"No, I do not," she said, playfully rolling her eyes.

Torin wasn't convinced. She knew her sister very well. "What's his name?"

"He's just a friend."

"That should have a name, yes?" Torin grinned.

Racquel leaned against the counter and sighed. "His name is Khysen. I just met him when I came back home."

"And he has you smiling like *that* already? Whew, honey," Mia sang.

It was like older sisters to be in her business in such a light-hearted, warming manner. Mia wasn't related by blood, but she was considered family for sure.

"Y'all take stuff so far," Racquel groused.

"Girl, please. We can ask about your little friend," Torin said just as another text from Khysen came through.

Racquel's eyes widened a bit as she read his message.

"Uh, oh. What's that look for?" Mia asked.

"He asked to pull up on me. What should I say?"

Torin adjusted the collar of Racquel's shirt. "Unless he's coming to work, tell him he can wait."

Racquel laughed. "He'd be a lovely model, thank you very much."

"Really? Let me see what he looks like."

Without hesitance, Racquel went to the Instagram app and pulled up Khysen's profile. He meant what he said when he told her to let him know when she made it home. Racquel surely thought he was just tossing his charm around, wanting it to seem like he cared, but he did. His name popped up in her notifications later that night as a new follower, and a message from him set in her inbox requests. They exchanged numbers and have been talking since.

"Oh. Okay." Torin grinned as she and Mia hovered over the phone on each side of her. "He's a cutie. Giving me 90's sitcom fine."

"Mhm. Male R&B lead singer cute," Mia agreed.

Racquel swiveled her head from one side to the other. "Okay, that's enough."

"Oop. I heard that." Mia snickered.

Torin waved her off. "How'd you meet him?"

Racquel cleared her throat. She didn't want to say and was honestly surprised that Synovi hadn't pillow-talked about what had gone down.

"A little get-together back in June," she answered.

"That's what's up. Tell him he can come through only if he plans to be a model. The one I booked had something come up."

Racquel's eyes brightened. "You for real?"

Laughing, Torin set up the next layout. "Yes. We can shoot some couple's content."

"We're not a couple, though."

Torin smirked. "Not yet. Tell him to come through. I can use this as a promo video at the awards."

All the finalists were given the opportunity to showcase their business in some form on the day of the award show. Getting into her marketing bag, Torin decided to shoot a mini commercial for the audience. While she rearranged a few things and spoke with Erin about how she wanted the last set to go, she propped her business phone up and went live on Instagram, being sure to tag her personal page. Every now and then, she gave her followers a glimpse of Kaine's Kitchen behind the scenes.

"Hey y'all," Torin spoke as followers tapped in. "It's content day for Kaine's Kitchen. Y'all swear all I do is stand in the front of the stove, so I had to show y'all what was up." She smiled, reading the comments.

locdwithleigh: *Hey friend! I need one of those jackets. It's real cute.*

The short-sleeved olive-green chef's coat was a new addition to her merch collection. What set it off was the double K gold embroidery logo and gold buttons.

"Thank you, girl. I got you. I'll get you one made with your logo on there," Torin responded to Leighton.

Having an entrepreneur as a best friend wasn't appreciated enough in Torin's eyes. Though in different fields, the two bounced ideas off one another, came up with business proposals, plugged each other's business, and so much more. Even if one of them wasn't an entrepreneur, the support would've still been the same.

Leighton understood her on a different level. Most days, if they knew what day it was, they didn't know if they were coming or going. Torin cherished their friendship most on those days when she was burnt out and an order away from giving up. She'd call Leighton to vent, and she'd let her. She could've been in the middle of a retwist, and Leighton would get Torin right on together.

It wasn't about the job title in their friendship but how they showed up in each other's lives. And when they couldn't, they gave each other grace because showing up for each other meant they had to show up and be present for themselves first.

They were ten minutes into the shoot when Khysen let Racquel know he was two minutes away. Making herself busy, she quickly walked over to the tripod the phone was on. She needed a quick distraction from the queasiness bubbling in her gut.

"Let me see who's on here," Racquel murmured, peeking at the phone.

Comments and floating hearts danced across the screen. She read a few and smiled big when she spotted a familiar username.

"Hey, brother." She grinned, acknowledging Synovi.

sblack_: *What's good, sis? Move yo' head so I can see your sister.*

"Y'all are too cute for me," she said, scooting out of the way.

On cue, Torin struck a pose while Erin captured a few photos. "Who?" she asked.

"You and Synovi. He told me to move out the way so he can see you."

Grinning like she'd heard the sweetest words, Torin came closer to the phone. She did a quick spin of her outfit, putting on a show for her man. The extra viewers had gotten lucky.

sblack_: *You look good, Love. Made a nigga's day seeing your face.*

Her hand flew over her mouth, concealing a cheeky blush. It was nothing for Synovi to pull that reaction out of her. He was talking as if she hadn't woken up to him this morning, but that was fine with her. Synovi didn't move or treat her like he had already made her his; he was forever shooting his shot.

"Thank you," she cooed. "Let me get back to work y'all. If you need any meals this week, I'm only accepting orders up until Thursday. Hey, Shonie. No, I'm not a food vendor at the awards this year. I'm a finalist," she said proudly.

Torin wasn't bragging, but even if she was, she had a right to. She moved with grace, though. Grateful and truly blessed to be in her position. Congratulatory comments poured in, and Torin thanked as many of them as she could before ending the live. Khysen strolled in seconds later.

"How y'all doing?" he spoke politely.

"Hey. We're good," Torin replied, sticking her hand out. "It's nice to meet you. I'm Torin, Racquel's sister. This is my assistant and friend, Mia, and Erin, our photographer."

The other women greeted him with waves. Khysen gave them a nod before focusing his attention on Racquel. A grin teased the corner of his mouth as she fidgeted under his gaze. He stepped her way, eliminating their distance.

"And, who are you? Can't be the girl who said she couldn't wait to see me."

Her face flushed with embarrassment at his call-out only they could hear. Racquel was no good under his charm nor the headiness of his cologne. Tucking a few dark brown tendrils behind her ear, she shyly greeted him.

"Hi."

Khysen smirked. "Can I get a hug?"

"Mhm." She hummed softly before lifting her arms

around his shoulders.

He pulled her into him by the waist and squeezed lightly before drawing back. Khysen took his time examining her modelesque frame as if they weren't on a schedule. He appreciated a woman with a nice figure, but Racquel's eyes captivated him more. Her trance-inducing, light brown orbs shaded by hybrid lash extensions and finely threaded brows told more than her voice would allow. Under his scrutiny, Racquel squirmed and licked her lips.

"What?" she wondered. "Why're you staring at me like I did something to you?"

"I'm just soaking up your energy. Appreciating you for letting a nigga in your space. That's coo' with you, Rocky?"

Racquel chuckled. "Yeah. That's fine. Just... quit looking at me like that," she said lowly.

"Oh, baby. Hurry up and wrap that conversation up," Torin interrupted. "I need that chemistry on camera."

The duo laughed and got to work. *Maybe coming home for the summer isn't that bad after all*, Racquel thought.

An hour later, Torin entered the SBCS building. Surprisingly, she'd gotten a boost of energy toward the end of the shoot. With the leftover food she hadn't sent with her crew of the day, Torin packed a little bit of everything into to-go containers for Synovi. Her impromptu visit was long overdue. The last time she brought him lunch in the middle of the day, he'd eaten her instead, claiming he'd wanted sweets all morning.

Torin didn't object, and now, she wanted a replay. Or even just some quality time. It was whatever with her. She could sit with him in complete silence, and that'd be just fine. Bypassing Eboni's closed office door, Torin made it to Synovi's and poked her head inside.

"Knock, knock." Her index knuckle rapped against the door.

Synovi's head lifted, and he smiled. "Look at you poppin' up on me."

Torin put her purse down in one of the chairs and sauntered to him. Rotating his chair, Synovi made room for her between his legs and accepted the loving kiss and hug she gave him. He rubbed up the back of her thighs, kneading the tension away before holding her tight. Torin melted.

"Mm. I needed this." She moaned with pure satisfaction.

Her hand stroked the back of his neck in a gentle calmness that made everything still around them.

"How'd the shoot go?" Synovi asked once she pulled away.

Her face lit up. "It went *so* good. I told myself I wouldn't go through any of the pictures tonight, but I lied."

They shared a laugh.

"Ion't know why you even set yourself up like that," Synovi said.

"Right. Anyway, are you hungry? I brought you some food."

Rounding his desk, she began pulling the containers out. The food was still warm, and his stomach rumbled at the delectable aromas. Standing, he told her he'd be right back and went to wash his hands in the connected restroom. When he returned, Torin had his food laid out with a fork and spoon sitting on a napkin.

"Thank you, Love," he said, with a kiss on her cheek before reclaiming his seat.

Before diving in, Synovi bowed his head and said grace. He scarfed down a turkey wing so fast that Torin couldn't help but laugh. From the first day she'd fed him, she took pleasure in fixing his plates and watching him eat.

"You must've been hungry," she commented, getting comfortable on the couch she added to his space for herself.

His head bobbed as he chewed rice smothered in gravy. "Starving."

"Glad I stopped by," she said and released a long yawn. "Whew. I just got sleepy out of nowhere."

"You were up super early. Lay down and get a nap in. I got a meeting in thirty minutes. When I finish eating, I'll rub your feet."

Torin whimpered at the sound of that. She'd been on them all week. Another yawn fell from her lips as she readjusted the pillow and stretched her body out.

"Okay," she mumbled tiredly.

A beat of silence fell around them before Synovi interrupted it.

"Love."

Torin peeled her eyes open. "Hmm?"

"I 'preciate and love you. I hope you know that. Feel that," he expressed.

She smiled softly. "I do, baby."

"Always?"

She nodded, hoping he felt her, too. "In all ways."

Torin loved Synovi in more ways than she could ever describe. Her genuine heart knew she'd be looking after his wounded one in whatever capacity he gave it. Fortunately for them both, Synovi presented it to her in ways she wasn't expecting but made it and him feel right at home. A physical place he could now call his own.

seven

If he had to guess, Synovi figured the level of pride he was experiencing was how most celebrities felt. He was far from famous, but being at the fifth Annual Kansas City People's Choice Awards made him feel like he was. From the private entrance for finalists only, the red carpet photos, and the reserved sitting area, the night had been nothing short of amazing.

This year, the event was held at the Myan Theater, and the city had packed it out with over one thousand guests. Tables for the food vendors were aligned in a designated walking space, and attendees stood shoulder-to-shoulder at the bar. There was only so much you could do to jazz up a theater, but the hosts of the night had the energy in the place on one hundred. It was an evening of celebration, and the crowd was doing just that. Especially, D'Marco.

"Aye, Torin," he said, leaning over to get her attention. "Take another shot."

She grimaced, eyeing the small clear cup with three fingers of tequila in it. "Give it to somebody else."

"Nah," he urged, passing the cup down the line of people.

Nikki, his girlfriend and child's mother, grabbed it before passing it over Lakisha to Racquel's outstretched arm. She bypassed Synovi and urged her sister to drink. D'Marco hadn't snuck the bottle in for no reason.

"C'mon, sis. You deserve another shot, award-winning chef," Racquel hyped.

Before intermission, Kaine's Kitchen was named the best catering service and food of 2023. The crowd went crazy when Torin accepted her award and gave a quick thank you speech. She'd blessed so many people's bellies with her meals, and they'd shown out for her tonight. She couldn't even make her way back to her seat without being stopped and congratulated.

"Right," Leighton chimed, who was sitting to her right. "Pour up, my girl!"

"Bae. Take one with me," Torin told Synovi.

He didn't drink, but tonight he was. D'Marco had his up already ready to go and handed it to him. Before they could toss them back, he felt a nudge to his shoulder from behind.

"I know y'all not taking a shot without me," GiGi said.

"Okay! I know that's right, GiGi. Let me pour you one up." Racquel laughed.

GiGi sat in the row behind them with Carolynn, Mr. K, Torin and Racquel's mama, Tracee, and her friend, and

Eboni, who sat in the aisle seat. Ms. Reid and her husband wanted to come, but she wasn't feeling her best. Still, she sent her love and support early that morning through text.

Drinks were poured and tossed back right before the announcer let everyone know the next award was about to be presented. The crowd settled, and music lowered as the hosts of the evening walked on stage.

"We added a new category to announce tonight instead of letting it roll across the screen. I didn't realize how important this service was until my wife broke it down to me. She said it had to be acknowledged, and y'all know what wifey says goes," Terrell said, making the crowd laugh.

"It most definitely is important," his co-host, Tish, voiced. "For those of you who don't always feel like cleaning up the house and just want to prop your feet up and have someone do it for you, this service is for you."

Synovi's stomach swirled with anxiety.

"And the nominees for best cleaning service are..."

Synovi zoned out. He didn't hear any of the other names being called. All of the long nights, disappointments, sacrifices, rejections, and accomplishments flashed through his mind. He was here, in this moment, right where he was supposed to be.

"And the 2023 KC People's Choice Award winner is... Synovi Black's Cleaning Service. Congratulations!"

Shouting and tugs of his arm around him broke his reverie. Earlier in the week, he joked around about writing out an acceptance speech if he won, and now that the time was here, he was stuck.

"Yes, siiiir, my boy!" D'Marco clapped proudly.

"Babe, oh my gosh," Torin squealed.

Their entourage had their phones out recording, capturing the business name plastered on the screen. Synovi stood to his feet with his heart racing. He couldn't believe it. Looking over his shoulder, he swallowed hard.

He didn't have to say anything for Torin to know he wanted her by his side. She took his awaiting hand, and they made their way down the aisle. Cameras flashed, and applause resounded as they ascended the steps to the stage. Proudly, with tears in her eyes, Torin stood back and let her man shine as he stepped up to the mic.

Synovi thanked the host and grabbed his plaque. He squinted as he stood center stage. The beaming lights damn near blinded him. Seeing the mass crowd from this view made his chest tight, but he pulled himself together.

He chuckled out of nervousness and cleared his throat. "I'ma little nervous, so excuse me," he said. His voice held a deep rumble of emotions he couldn't place.

"That's all right, baby! Take your time," a lady in the front row encouraged.

Synovi nodded, and his speech commenced. "First, I wanna thank God for even allowing me to be in this position."

"I know that's right!" came from multiple people in the crowd.

"I'm standing in answered prayers. 'Preciate everyone who voted for us. Especially our clients. We're a new business just getting our foot in the door, but we gon' keep it open. This cleaning service wouldn't be as successful without my staff, so thank y'all for working hard."

Synovi wasn't sure what'd come over him, but he spoke his next words with the confidence of a man who had been through it all and fought his way out of that dark tunnel. Someone out there needed to hear him.

"It's important to have people in your life who see the greatness in you when you can't. Cherish them, folks. Listen to 'em and trust the process. I'm a young Black man who came from the struggle. Built this business from the ground up, and now we're here."

Shouts and claps echoed throughout the theater.

"I'ma get off these people's stage." He chuckled. "But I wanna thank my GiGi, Ms. Reid, my sis, Racquel, D'Marco, my assistant, Eboni, Unique, Bostyn, Ayce, and the woman who helped jump-start everything."

Synovi glanced over his shoulder at Torin and gave her a light smile. He damn near got caught in a trance and became speechless again at the sight of her. Torin's burnt orange, floor-length satin dress hugged her generous curves just right, while a high left split displayed her thick thigh. The sleeveless halter style showed a sliver of her midsection and accentuated her snatched waist with the clinched material.

Moo had hooked her hair up in dramatic, voluptuous, wavy curls that stopped in the middle of her back. Silver stilettos graced her feet while diamonds sparkled in her ears, on her wrists, and ankle. They paired perfectly with the Cuban link chain around Synovi's neck. It was a gift to him over the weekend, and tonight was the perfect night to wear it. He had it tucked under his suit shirt for now. His black suit fit his broad frame so deliciously good that Torin couldn't wait to see his closet filled with more.

"Thank you isn't enough, but I'ma keep telling you. When I pray and thank God for the people in my life, I thank Him twice for you. It's whatever for you and about you, baby. Know that."

Everyone cooed as he openly expressed his love and gratitude without shame. Synovi held up his plaque, watching as the tears she tried to contain threatened to ruin her makeup.

"You know we had to double the awards, Love. Y'all be sure to book her and eat good. Thank you again, KC."

Finally done with his speech he pulled out of thin air, Synovi exited the stage.

"Man, I thought we were going to have to start playing music over you," Terrell joked. "Give it up one more time for that young man. I already know that's a monthly bill some of us husbands are about to have."

"Mhm. Us women, too," Trish agreed. "KC! Y'all ready to keep the show going?"

Synovi was cool with that. Backstage, Torin greeted him with open arms and the biggest smile. His head lowered to kiss her lips before he stood upright.

"What did I tell you, huh?" She grinned, playfully punching his chest. "I'm so damn proud of you."

Synovi smiled bashfully. "Thank you, baby. I wouldn't be holding this if you hadn't tricked me into coming to your crib that day."

"Tricked you!" She giggled heartily. "Boy, please.

Let's not go there with how this relationship really got here."

Smirking, Synovi pulled her into another hug around the waist. People brushed by them, but they were in their own little world.

"This shit belongs to both of us," he said.

Torin shook her head. "No, it does not. You earned that. Deserve that. This is your winning season. It was already mapped out before I entered your life."

"You just enhanced that mothafucka, huh?" Synovi smirked.

"Mhm. I'd like to think so. It's a lot of love residing in it now."

He kissed her lips again and squeezed her ass. "Keep giving me that shit, too."

Torin had no plans on stopping.

On the way to their seats, Projex, a well-known Grammy award-winning producer and songwriter from the city, stopped him. Loriana, his wife, was right by his side. She gave Torin a friendly hug and congratulated her. They'd never be too busy to come through to show love and support.

"Okay! Congratulations!" Loriana beamed.

"Thank you."

"What's good wit' it?" Projex said, and he and Synovi slapped hands. "Congratulations to both of y'all. My wife got a lil' too excited when you won. I had to come see what the fuck was going on," he jested.

Synovi chuckled, not the least bit offended. He'd be on the same type of time.

"Respect and 'preciate that. We're just out here

building generational wealth and memories," Synovi replied.

"I feel that," Projex said.

"All I know is that you're about to get booked like crazy, so how do we get a specialty service?" Loriana wanted to know. "I refuse to lose my spot on the calendar."

With two kids, running a business, and traveling, her cleaning days were no longer her ministry if they didn't have to be. She'd booked SBCS twice already and wasn't trying to miss out. Hiring a cleaning service was so convenient, and at this stage in her life, she was all for convenience.

"We gon' make sure you stay on there. Ain't nothing a lil' readjusting can't fix," Synovi said.

"Straight up. Celebrate y'all wins tonight and be safe," Projex said as he was summoned by someone.

"Y'all too," Synovi replied.

The women hugged, and they parted ways. Before they made it from behind the stage to their people, Synovi looked upward and closed his eyes.

"Thank you."

That was all he said and all He needed him to say.

Today solidified his decision to stop playing small. There would be nothing but big boss moves in his life regarding all aspects of it moving forward.

eight

```
What time will you be home?
I need to be the first one
to see that haircut lol.
```

Parked outside of *Kutz* Barbershop, Synovi read the text from Torin and smirked. She knew he was about to get his hair cut and didn't have time for him to be trying to run some fake errands so he could show it off. Torin wasn't insecure by any means and was very secure in their relationship. The youthfulness of it and its playful banter kept it fresh.

"This girl is crazy," Synovi mumbled.

"What'd you say?" Unique's voice sounded through the speakers of his truck.

He'd almost forgotten they were on the phone. With her future no longer up in the air, Synovi's optimistic mood about their relationship growing stronger in person dwindled. He didn't let that deter him from experiencing the woman Unique was or the mother she was striving to be. Like before, their situation was circumstantial. Their bond wasn't.

"Nothing. Reading this text from Torin," Synovi replied. "What were you saying?"

In like an hour. I'ma call
you on my way there.

"Tell her I said hi. And I was letting you know I got my pictures of y'all at the awards. My baby looked sharp!" Unique praised, making his lips curve upward.

"Thank you. That was my first time wearing a suit."

"Really? Well, don't make it your last. You were up on that stage looking like money." She chuckled, making him do the same.

"I felt like it."

His phone vibrated with another text popping up on the screen.

No. Call as soon as you
remove that cape! Lmao. I'm
just playing. See you in a
lil bit.

"And you should. I'm *so* proud of you, Synovi."

He could never get used to hearing those words from Unique, but he liked how they made him feel.

Wanted.

Seen.

Cared for.

Loved.

For so long, he brushed off accepting all the things a mother's love should feel like. There was no breaking or bending Unique regardless of what trials came her way. She overcame more challenges than anyone she knew and was grateful Synovi had been much more forgiving than this cruel world.

"Thank you, Mama," Synovi replied, and she gasped.

She couldn't mask her shock if she tried.

"Mama..." she mused. "I can get used to hearing you call me that."

Synovi chuckled. "Yeah. Calling you Unique doesn't seem right anymore."

The day after the awards, he watched videos of the speech he gave and cringed at the way he acknowledged her. Their relationship had grown past a first-name basis.

"I won't object to that. I'ma get on off here and call your granny," she said.

Synovi unlocked his truck. "A'ight. I need to get up there and see you soon."

"I'd love that. It's been more than a few months, but it's okay. I know you have a lot going on."

Unique never wanted to feel like a burden. As if coming to see her was a priority. Synovi nixed all her assumptions in the bud.

"Not that much that I can't make time. I'ma be that way soon."

She smiled. "Okay. I can't wait to see you, baby. Enjoy the rest of your day, okay? I love you."

"Love you too."

The call ended, and Synovi pushed the driver's door open and hopped out. Sliding his phone inside his pocket, he headed toward the entrance. He felt like he hadn't had a haircut in months with how busy he'd been. Loriana wasn't lying when she said they were about to be booked like crazy. The day after the awards, Eboni's emails and phone were flooded with inquiries and bookings. His employees gladly picked up extra shifts, and the job listings for new cleaners tripled.

That was a good problem to have, so if that meant he couldn't get to the barbershop for a few weeks, Synovi was fine with that. He was going to handle his business before anything. As he went to open the door, it was being pushed open. Holding it, he allowed the woman and a younger boy to walk out.

"Thank you so—" Her words faltered at the sight of him.

The young boy walking ahead of her stopped when he realized his mama wasn't right behind him. "Mama, come on. We gon' be late."

Ignoring him, she found the courage to speak. "Um, hey, Synovi," Simone muttered.

"What's good?" He spoke his words with a questioning tone as if to ask how she knew him.

Simone picked up on it right away.

"I'm, um, Jade's sister, Simone," she offered nervously.

"Okay."

His deadpan reply twisted her gut. A sense of foreboding washed over him, waiting for her to speak again. He'd experienced too much bad in his life not to know when it was around the corner.

"Aye. What's up? You got something you need to say to me?" Synovi questioned.

His harsh tone reminded her of who he really was and had been to her sister, and Simone let the ball drop.

“Yeah, I do. Jade passed away last month.”

Simone didn’t just drop the ball; she launched the mothafucka right upside his head.

What the fuck? Synovi thought.

“From alcohol poisoning,” Simone added.

Her revelation disconcerted Synovi in a way he didn’t expect it to. His chest tightened, seeing her eyes mist with the type of sadness that gutted you. Simone didn’t even want to utter those words to him. She hadn’t expected to see him. Ever.

“Damn,” Synovi mumbled. “I’m sorry to hear that.”

He truly was. Before Jade introduced her nutty side and he lost all respect and feelings for her, Synovi did rock with her heavy. She’d meant something to him. Something more than she ever should’ve. He wasn’t a heartless person, so hearing that she passed triggered his emotions some.

Now he knew why her calls and stalkerish behavior hadn’t presented itself in a while. The last time she’d reached out was the night of the awards. They were out at the afterparty celebrating when she blew his line down. Synovi accidentally answered one of the calls, and she rambled on and on about how she deserved him. Jade was furious watching him openly show love to Torin in front of all those people. In her mind, like Leighton said, if she couldn’t have him, she damn sure didn’t want Torin to be the lucky one. Three days later, she was gone.

“Yeah.” Simone sighed. “It happened out of nowhere.

I mean, I knew she was spiraling ever since her husband was killed, but I didn't know it was that bad."

The guilt of Omar's death had eaten Jade alive. Not just his death but the ending of everything else in her life. Synovi didn't care about that man, so he didn't bother to show any sympathy. Who he did care about, though, were his sisters.

"Where the girls at?" he questioned.

Simone wasn't expecting him to ask about them, but she was glad he had.

"They're with one of my cousins right now. I wasn't prepared to run into you today, and I feel so bad that I didn't reach out sooner."

"Wasn't no need for you to. Me and your sister cut ties a while ago."

Simone swallowed hard. "Yeah, and that's why I haven't been able to wrap my mind around all this. Her dying and then just... Listen..." She sighed. "When you get a chance, you should probably read the will she left behind."

Synovi frowned. "What the fuck for?"

"Just... check your mail in a few days. That's all I can say right now," she said before hurriedly walking off.

"Aye!" Synovi yelled. "Simone!"

His shouts went ignored as she rushed to get inside her car. Dumbfounded, Synovi stood there and watched as she peeled away from the curb, burning rubber. Whatever Jade left behind in her will had Simone shaken up, and Synovi was in no rush to find out why or why he specifically needed to read it. He wanted no parts. Some things were better left alone.

synovi & torin

Curiosity had gotten the best of him.

Or, maybe it'd been the pressure Torin applied that made Synovi have her call up Rianne, their lawyer, to meet. It'd been a little over a week since he ran into Simone, and Synovi had moved oddly since. Torin picked up on his disconnect immediately. He wasn't ignoring her or anything, but she noticed how he'd stare off in the middle of a conversation and was unable to hold eye contact with her when she asked what was wrong.

Torin was going to leave it alone before she hit him with some reverse psychology and ignored him until he talked, but was glad she didn't have to go to those lengths. Playing with his emotional state like that would never be her thing. They healthily communicated, so she waited it out, and Synovi brought it up to her.

That was two nights ago while they lounged on the couch and Synovi massaged her feet.

This afternoon, they were seated in Rianne's office with their hearts in their throats.

Synovi was numb.

His comprehension skills were stellar, yet nothing he read minutes prior made sense. Asking for clarification would only confirm how fucking selfish he already knew Jade was. This level of inconsideration had taken the fucking cake, though.

Torin was stunned to silence, but she needed

answers and had so many questions. She didn't want to overstep her boundaries. The subject was far too touchy. Thankfully, she didn't have to.

"So, that means they're my responsibility for life?" The apprehension in Synovi's voice made Torin's heart spasm.

Rianne sighed. She hated this for them. "Just until they're eighteen. You can always contest it, but we'd have to find valid legal reasons. Based on what we've read, you are the next of kin. This is a self-proving will, so there was no undue influence."

"Meaning there was no one there to persuade her of this decision?" Torin asked for clarification.

Rianne nodded. "Correct."

Synovi didn't regret much in life, but sleeping with Jade was one of them. Another regret was him responding to a message from Omar's mama, Claudia, a month after his death. She'd reached out in hopes of having a relationship with him. Synovi knew he'd never be open to that, but he used the opportunity to clear his lingering thoughts about who his biological father was.

It wasn't that he didn't believe his mama; Synovi just needed to know for himself. Optimistic about her future relationship with her grandson, whom she never knew about, Claudia agreed to submit a consent for DNA testing form. The court order was approved quickly, and the lab took two weeks to provide the results.

When he received them after handling his part of the deal, Synovi ghosted her. To some, it may have seemed wrong, and he should've been upfront with his true intentions, but he saw no wrong in his actions. Not until now. Had he never confirmed Omar's paternity, Jade would've never been able to get him this easily. Even if she did list him as guardian, it wouldn't have been until now that he'd have to go through DNA testing to prove he was next of kin, and Synovi more than likely wouldn't have compromised.

His jaw ticked as he reread the paragraph of the letter that made him want to vomit.

To Whom It May Concern:

I, Jade Lewis, am writing this letter to inform anyone, including the court of proper probate jurisdiction, of my wishes in the event I should die while my children are minors, I would like Synovi Black of Kansas City, Missouri, to act as guardian of Skylar Lewis and Kalie Lewis.

"She can't do this shit, man," he grumbled, tossing the papers onto the desk. "This shit was drawn up months ago."

"As if she was planning it," Torin added.

Dying hadn't been in Jade's plans, but she felt like it inside. Tilting a bottle to her lips had been her getaway for so long. While she'd send the girls with her sister so she could indulge, most days, she didn't. Thankfully, the evening she was found unresponsive, the girls had been with Simone.

After overconsuming so much liquor in a short amount of time, Jade went to sleep far too intoxicated. In her sleep, she vomited without waking up, causing the contents to block her airways. Since she wasn't positioned in a recovery position, she suffocated to death. It was tragic, and Simone had been losing her mind since.

She'd already been barely holding it all together when she came across Jade's will. Simone was listed as the executor, forcing more responsibility on her while she grieved and took care of her nieces. Then, she read the letter of guardianship, and her entire heart crumbled. Not just for her nieces but for Synovi as well.

Rianne wanted to give her *real* opinion on what she thought, but that was not what she got paid to do. She'd witnessed many cases where guardianship was placed upon people unprepared for the role, but there wasn't much they could do. Especially when another person of interest wasn't listed as a potential guardian in the event the first one didn't accept or was unable to fulfill the wishes.

"It is unfortunate, but it's basically written in stone. We can try to contest it if that's something you want to do," Rianne said.

"I need to call her. Did Simone leave her contact information anywhere?" Synovi asked.

He felt it was better to do this in front of a lawyer just in case. Torin grabbed the papers Rianne printed off the desk and flipped through them. Simone didn't leave her contact, but Jade did. It was protocol. Punching the number into his keypad as Torin called it out, Synovi listened to the phone ring with bated breaths. Simone answered on the fourth ring.

"Hello?"

"Simone, this Synovi. You got a minute?"

Reaching for the remote, she turned the TV down, quieting her background. "Hey, yeah. I do. I take it you read the will."

"I did, and what the fuck, man. Did you know she put this in here?"

"No," she spoke firmly. "The only time we've ever discussed her will was when she listed me as the guardian."

"So, when did she change this shit? Y'all got into it or something? I mean, what made her make me, out of all people, the one she'd want to take care of her kids? What type of sick shit is that?"

Torin rubbed his arm, coaxing him to keep his anger at this level. She could tell he was about to fly off the hinges. Sighing, Simone shook her head on the other end. His rapidly asked questions didn't catch her off guard because she had the same ones. But she knew why Jade did what she did.

"We didn't see eye to eye when Omar was killed. A few words had been exchanged about what he'd done to your mother, and she tried defending him. I didn't. I never thought she'd take our disagreement this far, though."

"That's... that's fucked up," Synovi said, processing her words. "And she never mentioned it to you?"

"Nope. I'd still get the girls, take them to school and everything. I'm just as confused as you are, but I know my sister." She sniffled.

"What you mean?"

"She did this out of spite. Maybe jokingly, but in her mind, it was some type of payback. She wanted to hurt you like you hurt her. I love my sister so much, but she's always had a motive when doing things. This tops them all, though."

Torin's nostrils flared with hatred, listening to her speak. She had called it long before now that Jade wasn't a good person, and this only solidified her opinion more.

"It does. She thought I ruined her life, so she's trying to ruin mine," Synovi concluded. "Let me dump my kids off on him since he wouldn't be with me."

His pissed-off chuckle gave the women goosebumps.

"Yeah, basically. I've been doing okay with taking care of them, but I'm struggling," Simone said with sadness. Her voice shook as she spoke. "I'm grieving so badly trying to take care of myself, my son, my mama, and my nieces."

Synovi felt a pang of sadness for her, but it didn't outweigh his frustration. "Is that why you were shocked to see me the other day?"

"Yes. I know I should've reached out to you when I first read her will, but I couldn't bring myself to do it. Not when I knew how the information inside would flip your world upside down again. You don't deserve that," Simone said.

She was conflicted and heartbroken. Her attempt to hide that he was now Skylar and Kalie's guardian had failed. Everything in her wanted to contest Jade's will, but she knew her sister wanted the girls to have a relationship with him. Probably more than she wanted the relationship with Synovi. It was all Jade talked about, and Simone had grown tired of hearing it. That was when Jade removed her as their emergency contact at the school and summer program.

Jade was moving maliciously for shock value and shits and giggles and left a disaster in her demise. Simone also knew that Jade didn't like Torin, so she made her decision with the spiteful intent to tarnish their relationship.

Stressed, Synovi sat back in his chair and squeezed his eyes shut. His headache that morning had morphed into an eye-blurring migraine with all of this news.

"You can always refuse," Simone said softly. "I really hope you don't, though."

As selfish as she didn't want to be, Simone was exhausted. She hadn't known an inkling of peace since Jade began to spiral. With her own things going on in her life, Simone hadn't balanced basically being a mother to three kids. So, though it wasn't fair for Jade to grant Synovi guardianship, she didn't find it fair to have to step up in such a way, either. Especially at such a young age.

Like her late husband, Jade had crossed too many family members for Simone to even consider placing Skylar and Kalie in their care. Their mother had already agreed with Jade's decision, so she was out of the question. Now, Simone hoped Synovi could find it in his heart to accept his new role. If not, Simone knew she'd soon be spiraling, free-falling, just like her sister.

"I need some time to think. I'll hit you back soon," Synovi told her.

"Okay. Whatever is best for the girls. I know this is a lot, but I'm trying to think about the best outcome for them. You wouldn't be in this alone."

As she hung up, Simone hoped her parting words left a mark. They sat in silence for almost a minute until Rianne spoke up. She had another appointment soon and couldn't be late.

"It's a lot. Too much to make a decision right now. When and if you decide to take on guardianship, let me know. We can go over everything again."

Synovi stood up. "A'ight. I 'preciate you for squeezing us in."

"Of course. Please, take care of yourself, okay? Don't feel burdened by someone else's choices. You'll have to live with them in the long run."

That was what Synovi was afraid of.

They exited Rianne's office and made it to Synovi's truck. He started the engine but hadn't bothered to pull off yet.

"You—"

"I'm—"

They spoke at the same time, needing to get some shit off their chests.

"Go ahead," Torin encouraged.

"I'm fucked up behind this."

Synovi bit into his bottom lip. Torin didn't speak, giving him the space he needed.

"If I accept being their guardian, I feel like I'ma be betraying not only myself but you and my mama."

"No, don't think that. That petty beef we had is nothing in comparison to this. What I feel about her doesn't matter. She never mattered. You are all I care about, and I'm going to be by your side with whatever choice you make."

Synovi swallowed hard. It sounded good right now, but he knew better.

"I know how the system is when you're a kid. Don't nobody really give a fuck until it's too late. Simone could let the state get involved because it's too much responsibility. I'd never be able to live with that knowing what I know."

Torin understood completely.

"There's also a possibility that she doesn't," she said.

"I should've never stopped responding to her texts." Synovi sighed.

Like Jade's calls, Skylar's texts had stopped as well. She hadn't stopped sending Synovi voice messages from her iPad; he ignored them. He couldn't keep torturing himself and now regretted it. Had he, he would've known before now that his sisters were motherless. Eager to know what some of her voice messages said, Synovi unlocked his phone. Scrolling, he came to the unread messages from the email address he had silenced alerts from.

There was a thread of them dating back to last month. He tapped one, and his heart lurched in his chest.

"Hi, brother! You said you didn't know if you'd see us again, but I've been good, like you said. I can't wait to ride in your truck again. Talk to you later!"

He pressed play on another message.

"It's me again. Why didn't you answer when I called you? I was tryna tell you about this girl at school. She said her brother could beat mine up, and I was like, un, un! Not mine. Answer the phone, big head!"

Her animated voice made him blow out a deep breath as he continued.

"Kalie wanted to say hi. Say hi before we get caught." Five seconds went by before Kalie's meek voice was heard. *"Hi."* Skylar took back over seconds later. *"You know you see our messages! If your phone is off, just say that. Bye!"*

They couldn't help but chuckle at that one, and they needed the lightheartedness because the last voice note crushed them to pieces.

"Brother." Skylar sniffled. *"I don't know what's going on. It's so much. My mama isn't alive anymore. My TT is sad and crying. I'm sad. She keeps saying everything is too much. I don't wanna be here. Can you come get us like you said? We'll be good."*

In the passenger seat, tears Torin didn't even know she produced dripped down her face. With a balled-up fist to his mouth, Synovi locked his phone.

"Fuck!" he shouted, teary-eyed.

They fell like the guard he'd been keeping up. Synovi broke down in the driver's seat of his truck, knowing exactly what he had to do. His heart, the one he'd worked so hard on opening, wouldn't allow him to do anything else. His sisters needed him like he'd always needed someone.

nine

"I know you didn't come over here to mope around all day," Tracee said, stepping into the living room and eyeing her daughter.

Laid out on her mother's couch with a plush throw blanket from Fancy Homebody draped over her, those were Torin's exact plans. She'd been at her home all evening, lounging around with a heavy heart.

"I'm not moping," she whined.

Tracee took a seat where her feet rested. "Hmm. So, what do you call it?"

Ending her day early, Torin abandoned all duties and came straight to the person she knew she could vent to without feeling bad. She had her friends, but she needed some advice that only a mother could give. It'd been a week since they met with Rianne, and Torin still couldn't wrap her brain around what transpired. Not just during their meeting but afterward as well.

"I'm torn," Torin confessed. "Imagine you and your boyfriend living y'all's best lives, and then in the blink of an eye, he becomes a guardian to his little sisters. I don't know what to do."

"You want to break up with him?"

Torin sat up so quickly that she saw stars. "No."

Her answer was direct and clear-cut.

"Okay, so what do you mean by not knowing what to do? Your role as his girlfriend hasn't changed."

Torin despised and loved when Tracee made her really think about the questions she asked. She wasn't getting any of that surface-level conversation over here. If she wanted to talk, Tracee would make her do just that.

"But it will. He'll have sole responsibility for them, shifting all dynamics of his life."

"And you're afraid you'll no longer fit in it."

It wasn't a question but an observation. Torin's fearful thoughts fleeted through her eyes and face.

She sighed. "In a way, yes."

"So, he decided to get them?"

"Yes. Simone is supposed to drop them off on Sunday," Torin answered.

Meeting with Rianne and the phone call with Simone wasn't the reason Synovi made up his mind about being their guardian. Skylar's voice notes had him dialing Simone's number on their way to the crib. Their phone call lasted over an hour, and by the time they hung up, arrangements for the girls to move in had been made.

She tossed the cover from her frame as her skin grew warm. "Does it make me selfish that I'm not ready to take on that huge responsibility with him? Because it won't just be him that I'm worried about anymore.

Those girls will need me, too, but what if I can't show up in the way they deserve?"

"Selfish? Not at all. It shows you're human. Of course, you aren't ready to step into that role, but is anyone ever ready? It's a lot. He can't just give his sisters back, and even if he does, they're still a huge part of his life now."

"I know he is. It's all he's been talking about this week." Torin sighed. "I've been kind of distant with him, and now I feel bad because I know running away from the situation won't help it any."

"It won't," Tracee agreed.

"And I lied, telling him I'd be by his side with whatever choice he made."

Tracee chuckled lightly. "Did you lie, or did you just get scared?"

"Both. Look where I'm at." Torin huffed, leaning her head against the back of the couch. "I didn't disappear completely. I got the girls's room all fixed up and changed the guest bathroom to a girly theme. I just haven't been staying over there. He isn't pressuring me to do anything, but I can tell he knows what I'm feeling. He always does."

"You need to tell him how you feel. I know you love him."

"So much," Torin added.

She didn't just love him; Torin was deep in love. Immersed in Synovi Black to the brim of her lower eyelids because she still needed to see him and give him her light. Give him all her *love*.

"And loving someone means caring for them in ways *they* need to be cared for. Providing them with a space that only *you* can provide. It doesn't mean you have to silence your wants and needs. That's not how relationships should work."

Torin breathed in a stuttered breath as her eyes misted. Tracee grabbed her hand and rubbed it soothingly.

"You have such a pure heart, honey. The fact that you're concerned about being enough for them proves how selfless you are. I won't lie to you and say that you won't be making some sacrifices, but it's all about compromising, too. Synovi didn't just consider y'all's relationship enough to involve you in everything, but he also factored in the way you feel. He didn't just spring this on you and force you to accept his new reality."

Torin didn't bother to wipe the tears she was shedding. She'd been an emotional wreck all week, only having her mother to confide in about her reservations. There was so much to consider, but not being there wasn't an option. Sniffling, she lifted her head.

"I want to be there. I'm afraid that if I become attached to those little girls and we don't work out, I have to let them go. That's what happened between me and Don."

It was never about not being there for Synovi and the girls. She'd thought about the bond she and DJ, Don's son, had built and how it was practically non-existent now. It hurt her to set those boundaries with his family because she loved them, but subjecting herself to discomfort for the sake of history would hurt more.

"You can't compare your past to something that

hasn't happened yet, Torin. What was it you told me people hold on to?"

Her chest hiccuped as she sniveled.

"The good things they know they can keep, not have to give back," she answered solemnly.

"Exactly. You had to let Don, his sister, and anyone attached to him go for your peace. So, unless you plan on breaking up with him and going on about your business, figure out how to come to some common ground without inflicting more pain on one another. I'm sure he isn't trying to let you go because he took on another role in his life. That's a man standing on business and determined to break generational curses. If I can be honest, I'm certain he'd do it without you, but he *knows* he doesn't have to. You know it, too."

Tracee had just said a mouthful. Standing, she kissed her daughter's cheek.

"Thank you, Mommy," Torin said softly.

"Always, my baby. Now, get up off my couch and go home to your man. I'm sure he misses your presence."

Torin knew he did because she missed his, too. That much was proven when an incoming call from Synovi came through while she was on her way to his condo. Her stomach rumbled with an overwhelming sense of guilt and avidity to hear his voice.

"Hey," she answered, switching lanes.

"What's up, Love? Where you at?"

His question made her toes tingle.

"On my way to you."

"Bet. I was hoping that's what you were going to say," he said.

"Why? What's the matter?"

There was no urgency in his words, but she couldn't help but worry.

"Nothing I'm trying to discuss over the phone. I'll see you when you get here."

"Okay," Torin forced out. She wanted to throw the fuck up. "I'll be there in a little bit."

Synovi told her a'ight and hung up. As badly as she wanted to make a U-turn and head back to her mama's house, Torin knew she had to face the music.

And that was exactly what she walked into thirteen minutes later. The melodic voice of Ginuwine singing "I'm In Love" crooned through the wireless speaker and greeted her ears as she entered the garage. Next to entice her senses was the delicious smell of food. She dropped her purse and keys in the foyer and made her way deeper into the house.

Her heart warmed, noticing the made-up dinner table and lit candle on the island. Synovi turned to greet her, and she lost her train of thought. He stood before her, looking finer than fine, in black jeans and a crisp white Polo tee.

A single rose rested in his left hand as he held the stem of a wine glass with her favorite wine in his right. The handsome smirk on his face ruined Torin's panties. She loved his low-cut waves and sittable face. Some days, she'd get caught staring, but he never seemed to mind.

"I'ont like when you go missing on me," Synovi acknowledged, invading her space.

He used her words on her and kissed her cheek.

Torin's head fell back, allowing him to kiss her exposed neck. Synovi gripped her ass, and she trembled at his touch and the heady smell of his Dior Homme cologne. Torin wanted to climb him.

"Glad you came home, though," he added, smiling a little. The expression displayed in his eyes and on his face. He handed her the glass. "You hooked the girls's room up."

"You like it?" Synovi nodded. "Thank you," she said, then accepted the rose. "Only one?"

"Yeah. You'll get the rest when you tell me where you've been at. I ain't just talking about today, either."

Torin took a generous gulp of her wine. "Okay."

"I'ma feed you, too. Gotta make sure you well fed for the night."

She grinned bashfully behind the rim of the glass, knowing exactly what he meant. Synovi had the stamina of a professional swimmer in the bedroom, keeping his masterful strokes long and wide until the very last lap.

"You cooked?"

"I did a lil' something." He chuckled. "I ain't you, though, so don't be trying to clown me."

Torin giggled. "Never. I'm sure I'll enjoy it. Thank you," she said, taking a peek inside the pots. His act of love was so endearing, and Torin didn't feel like she deserved it with the way she'd been acting. None of that mattered to Synovi. Only this moment did.

"You wanna eat or address the tension in the room first? I'm only asking 'cause I care about what you want from me."

Swallowing the lump in her throat, Torin placed her

glass on the counter before it slipped from her suddenly sweaty grasp.

"I want this. I want us," she stated.

"I want you and us, too, but if you trying to be done with a nigga and let me off easy, let me know. I'm too much for you?"

His question was asked in the most self-assured way that Torin's knees buckled. *Damn, I love him,* she thought to herself.

"No. I know why you'd think that," she replied.

"'Cause that's how you making it seem, but I know you, baby."

He stepped her way again, and Torin licked her lips as her heart raced.

"Talk to me," he urged.

"I'm scared. I don't know who or what you want or expect me to be in your life right now. I keep second-guessing if I'm doing enough or doing too much. I don't like going missing on you, either, but it's been a challenge sorting my emotions out. You have enough going on, and I'd just be adding my emotional stress on you." She breathed, done rambling.

Synovi gripped the bottom of her face and forced her to stare at his darkened pools of gentleness and understanding.

"Listen to me. I want, nah, I need you to be what you've always been in my life. My light. My Love. That beam of life when shit gets gloomy. Ain't nothing gon' change between us just because the circumstances have. I'm not asking you to change, baby. I swear, I'm not."

"You don't have to. It's inevitable." Torin sniffled.

These fucking tears. Ugh! she thought.

"How?"

"Because... there's no way I can't love something that's a part of you and dear to your heart. I just know I'm going to love those girls with everything in me and be sick to my stomach if we don't work out."

Synovi frowned. "Where am I going?"

"Huh?"

"I said, where the fuck am I going? The only way this shit won't work out is if I leave, and why would I do that? You're the best thing that has ever happened in my life, and I love the fuck out of you. I don' been through the worst of the worst; nothing can alter the foundation we have. That shit is built on solid ground, Love. It might shake a lil' bit, knock some shit over, but that comes with the territory. You can't run every time a shift happens. Stand ten toes in it with me 'cause I'm not gon' ever make you pick up the pieces alone."

Torin's bottom lip poked out, letting his words penetrate her soul. His words comforted her like a hot mug of her favorite tea from *Flyest*. He was never too wrapped up in himself to cater to her emotional needs, even when she struggled to express them. Weaving his fingers through her hair, Synovi pulled her against his chest and massaged her scalp. He felt the dampness of his t-shirt immediately.

"Shhh. I hate when you cry. That shit makes my fucking stomach hurt."

In the midst of her breakdown, Torin couldn't help but laugh at his insolent comment. Synovi meant no harm and would soothe any of her pain away in a millisecond.

"I'm sorry," she whimpered, fluttering her eyes up at him.

Synovi kissed her forehead. "For crying?"

"No, for—"

"Don't. Never apologize for how you feel or for telling me. I'm your man. If you can't come to me, you can't go to nobody. I don't want you to anyway. Tell me all your secrets, a'ight? All your fears, too."

Torin giggled as he wiped her eyes. Drowning her in affection like only Synovi could.

"All of them?"

"Yeah." He smirked. "I'll keep them shits locked away in my heart, and you the only one who got that, so they gon' stay confidential."

Torin snickered. "What a way with your words, Mr. Black. You must want something from me, talking like this."

"Shit, I do," he said, lowering his lips to her ear. They grazed her earlobe, and Torin shuddered.

"What do you need?" she asked breathlessly.

"For you to eat, so I can eat you and show you how much I missed you and my pussy," he spoke huskily and spanked her ass. "C'mon."

Her eyes widened as he stepped away from her and washed his hands at the sink.

"Really? You can't show me right now? I'm horny," she whined.

Synovi laughed loudly, making Torin's heart swell with pure adoration.

"I'ma give you some dick, Love. Make you beg for this shit, too. Let me show you GiGi raised me right first."

Torin smiled. "I mean, okay. I guess I'll let you do that."

"Yeah. Let me. And you better make up for all the days you stayed at home and not in my bed this week."

Her spine tingled and clit thumped. She had three days of making up to do and knew Synovi would make her regret every one she missed.

Sunday had rolled around quicker than any of them expected.

With his nerves on edge, but not as bad as he thought they'd be, Synovi paced around his condo, waiting for Simone to arrive.

"Will you sit down somewhere," GiGi fussed over the phone. He had called her on FaceTime twenty minutes ago and had been working her nerves since.

"Nah. I'm good," Synovi said.

Grabbing a Clorox wipe, he went over the spotless counter once more, and GiGi shook her head. He was trying to make a good second impression and was going the extra mile to do so. Not only had he and Torin stayed up late, stocking their room with clothes, shoes, accessories, and toys, but they got up this morning and went to the Apple store for new iPads. Simone let him know that Skylar had lost hers, and she'd been sad for weeks.

That was an easy fix for her big brother. He dropped a bag on them and hadn't flinched. Besides the materialistic things, Synovi hoped they could adapt to their new arrangements. He knew how he felt when moving from house to house while in the system, and no incentives were involved. Just fucking misery and broken promises.

"Well, stand still for a second. My goodness. You're making my head hurt with all this moving around. Feel like I'm on a boat." GiGi huffed.

Torin snickered in the distance before walking closer. She grabbed the phone from him. "Now, why are you doing all that?"

"Because y'all won't let me be there to meet my grandbabies but wanna call me every five minutes. What, I ain't good enough to meet them?"

Synovi exhaled and shook his head. Stubborn. That was what GiGi was, and he knew exactly where he'd inherited the trait.

"It's not that," Torin said. "He doesn't want to overwhelm them on the first day."

"Exactly. We can bring them by there once they get comfortable," Synovi added.

GiGi pushed her glasses up on her nose. "That's fine. I just feel left out, but I know it's for the best right now."

How she quickly stepped into her role as their grandmother without having even met them eased Synovi's worries a ton. GiGi was one of the most important people in his life, and there was no way he would've been able to do this if she had not accepted them. It was an easy decision when Synovi sat down and told her what was happening.

"Those babies ain't ask to be here in all this drama. Y'all are going to need all the support, and it takes a village. Always has. Of course, I'll help you out with them. I don't even know why you asked," GiGi said the day after he met with Rianne.

Synovi asked out of respect but should've known she would have his back. She always did. This time was no different.

"Look at you wanting to take over already. That's so sweet," Torin gushed.

"Hell, I need to do something. You don' stole my only grandson. I see Racquel more than I do him nowadays."

Synovi smirked. Their relationship was the funniest thing to witness, but he fucked with it heavy. GiGi had taken both Torin and Racquel under her wing with ease. There was enough of her to go around, and she made sure of it.

"You replaced me with her, but faking like I don't be popping up over there," he said, grabbing the phone back.

"Oh, boy, hush. Don't try to defend yourself now. What time is she bringing them by? It's a school night. Y'all gotta get them babies on a schedule."

That was a normal grandmother's response. GiGi would've had the girls bathed and in bed before they could blink. It was going on five in the evening, so Simone should've been pulling up any minute now. They waited until the beginning of a new month to officially move the girls, and Synovi was grateful for that. It gave everyone just enough time to get their ducks in a row and start the month of October off on a positive note. So, he hoped.

"In a few minutes," he replied.

"Well, all right. Call me tomorrow and let me know how everything goes. Everything is going to work out just fine. God is still in the blessing business, and those girls are one of them," she declared. "I love you."

"I love you, too, GiGi."

"My girl." Torin leaned into the lens. "You got this, too. You're a natural nurturer, so don't be over there worrying like you do. Send me some pictures, too," GiGi said.

"We will."

The call disconnected, and Torin exhaled loudly.

Synovi smirked. "You look more nervous than me."

"I was," she admitted with a tight smile. "I'm good now, though."

Torin rested her head against his chest, seemingly helping calm him with her touch. Synovi hugged her around the shoulders, not wanting to let her go. This was the stillness right before a brewing storm arrived.

"Our lives are about to change," Synovi admitted, rubbing her back.

"In the best way possible. You're such a good man."

Torin lifted her head and pecked his lips. Synovi smirked, making her stomach flutter with need.

"How good?"

Ego-stroking. She did it for him every time.

"Good enough to wanna make you a daddy."

His brow hiked upward. "Word? Shit, we can start right now."

Her head fell into his chest again as she giggled. “I’m joking. That’s my ovulation pussy talking.”

“Tell her to speak up, then. I’ont like shy pussy,” he joked, making Torin crack up.

“I’m not about to play with you.”

She removed herself from his embrace, and Synovi grabbed her hand.

“Aye. Thank you for being here. I know you sick of me telling you that, but I’m for real.”

Torin smiled softly. “I know, baby. There’s no other place I’d rather be.”

Those words shook his nerves away.

“We get to stay here forever?” Skylar questioned as they pulled into Synovi’s driveway.

Parking, Simone did her best to hold it together. “Yes. For now,” she said, glancing out of her window.

She spotted a pink four-wheeler and toys in the yard next door. That brought her a sense of relief, hoping the girls would at least have some kids their age to play with. They didn’t just want to spring their move on them on the day of, so Simone let them know they’d be staying with Synovi. Skylar had a million and one questions, and she did her best to answer them all. So far, she seemed excited.

Kalie just nodded and smiled when Simone explained their living arrangements. She never really knew how to get her to open up anymore, and she blamed herself but didn't need to. None of this was her fault, and she hoped her niece would grow out of the mute stage she was in.

"I'm excited," Skylar cheered, unfastening her seatbelt.

"Me too," Kalie whispered, following her lead.

Their excitement didn't do much to comfort Simone's bleeding heart as they grabbed some of their things from the trunk and backseat. All week, she'd been questioning whether she'd made the right choice or not. At her sister's wishes, she was practically handing over her nieces to a stranger. They'd agreed on Synovi keeping the girls throughout the week and her getting them every other weekend.

The schedule wasn't set in stone, but they'd test it out for a few weeks and go from there. Thankfully, they were mature enough to know that every decision they made would affect the girls's future, so it was crucial to make it beneficial. Simone had doubts, but they all washed away with the departing storm and looming clouds when Synovi opened the door before they could knock. He was just as anxious as they were.

"Brother!" Skylar squealed, dropping the belongings in her hand.

She took off running up the walkway toward him, almost knocking him over with the way she rushed his frame. Her skinny arms wrapped around his waist made Synovi feel the most vulnerable he'd ever felt. Little Skylar was testing his manhood, and Synovi was failing.

Especially when she started crying. Skylar hugged him tighter, and his heart broke.

"Hey, hey," he cooed, rubbing her back and squatting so they were face to face. "It's okay. Why you crying?"

Skylar shrugged. She didn't know what she was feeling right now, but she was emotional.

"I-I don't know. I guess I thought I wasn't ever going to see you again," she expressed. "It made me sad."

"I'm right here," Synovi said, staring into her wet, brown eyes. They were a drastically different hue than Kalie's. "I ain't going anywhere."

Her eyes twinkled with hope in his words, and Synovi was glad she didn't make him promise because that wasn't one he could keep if things ended up out of his control. A sigh of relief left him as Skylar hugged him again and said okay before pulling away.

"Don't tell anyone I was crying," she whispered.

He smirked and stood up. "I won't. Y'all got more stuff in the car?"

"Yes," Simone answered, clearing her throat. She told herself she wasn't going to cry, and there went Skylar, ruining her plans. Synovi headed down the walkway to retrieve the rest of their things, and Kalie hid behind Simone's leg as best as she could. Hurt masked his face immediately.

"Give her a second," Simone said in a hushed tone. "She just woke up."

He nodded and gave her a side hug. "A'ight. Let me get y'all stuff, and we can head inside."

Skylar made herself right at home, slipping her shoes off and reacquainting herself with Torin.

“I remember you,” Skylar said. “What was your name again?”

“It’s Torin. Your hair is different today. I love it.”

Skylar’s face lit up as she swung her braided ponytail from side to side. One thing Simone made sure of was keeping her nieces together. They never looked unloved or unkempt.

“Thank you! You see my heart? It’s cute, huh?”

“It is,” Torin agreed, chuckling. Skylar was too much, in a good way. The perfect entertainment they needed right now. The designed braid on the side of her head was something she saw and wanted to try, so Simone let her.

“I keep her hair in braids because it’s so thick,” Simone informed. “This one right here is way too tender-headed for them.”

She puffed out Kalie’s puffball.

“What’s up, baby girl?” Synovi spoke after taking their stuff to their room.

“My daddy used to call her that!” Skylar blurted, hopping into one of the barstools.

Simone wasn’t usually caught off guard by Skylar’s outbursts or inquisitive thoughts she couldn’t hold in, but this time was different. Her bewildered eyes shot toward Synovi, hoping her niece didn’t ruin the mood. She hadn’t at all, as Synovi steered the conversation with true adroitness.

“Yeah? Well, we gon’ have to find another nickname then. Ain’t that right?” He grinned at Kalie.

The women caught on to his shade and chuckled under their breaths. Synovi now knew why she asked how he knew Kalie's nickname in the truck that day. It was a moniker they hadn't heard in a while. Kalie's little feet moved her body in front of him, and she lifted her arms. Without second-guessing whether he should pick her up, Synovi swooped her into his arms.

"Oh, my gosh. You don't have to pick her up. She's four." Simone chuckled, heart full at the sight.

Synovi hugged her to him, and Kalie rested her head on his shoulder while hugging his neck. If nothing else confirmed that he'd made the right choice, this moment solidified it. Torin blinked back tears and excused herself to the guest half-bath for privacy.

"Love," Synovi called out.

Torin's chest stuttered as she met his loving eyes.

"Don't go missing."

Those three words made the tears fall. In his own personal way, Synovi let her know that he wanted her here. His actions always did. When she came out, they'd migrated to the living room as Synovi gave them a tour of the place. Kalie stayed glued to his side while Skylar talked Torin's ear off, which she didn't mind. They both left their sides when they reached the bedroom that was once considered Synovi's office.

"It's so pretty!" Skylar praised. "And I have my own bed."

She rushed toward the full-size bed and jumped on it.

"Un, un, Missy. You know better," Simone scolded.

"She good," Synovi intervened.

He'd done the same when he was finally given his own room at one of his foster homes. Simone shook her head. She knew they were about to have Synovi wrapped around their fingers. Kalie's wide, mysterious eyes scanned the room. Torin opted for a neutral, soft tone with a light blush pink, cream, and brown color scheme. Floral wallpaper in the same colors was on the wall where their cream, upholstered bedframes rested. They matched the other walls. A fifty-inch TV had been hung up above a white ten-cube organizer. In another corner sat a brown desk for them to do their homework.

"Y'all... y'all did this in that short amount of time?" Simone asked.

Synovi nodded and lowered Kalie, who wiggled to be put down. "Yeah. Torin ordered some designers to come through."

"You a real one," Simone commented, facing Torin. "I know you and my sister had y'all issue, but I want you to know I have no problem with you at all. It takes a real woman to step up in the way you have, so thank you. But please don't make me have to whoop some ass if you mistreat them in any way."

Torin would've been offended had she been lesser of a woman, but she wasn't.

"I would never. I have no malice in my heart toward those little girls, not even you. My only concern is making sure they and their brother receive the utmost love over here. We're a team, not enemies."

Simone nodded and blinked her watery eyes. "Got you."

"And, I got you. I meant to ask you, are they allergic to anything? I'ma cook dinner in a few. You're welcome to stay."

Synovi exhaled with relief, seeing them not butt heads. They hadn't been over the phone all week, but it was a different story in person. As they busied themselves with what the girls could and could not eat, Synovi walked over to their desk and leaned against it.

"You like y'all's room?"

"I love it!" She threw herself into him for a quick hug. "Thank you! I knew you'd come and get us. I told Kalie you were busy."

Synovi glanced at Kalie, who leaned against his leg. "What about you? You like your room?"

"Yes," she spoke softly, making Synovi's eyes widen.

He smiled big, happy to hear her voice. Looking across the room, he and Torin made eye contact as Simone scrolled through her phone to pull up something.

I love you, Torin mouthed, grinning.

I love you more, Synovi mouthed back.

They'd been nervous for no reason. In the end, love always wins, no matter the circumstances.

ten

Torin had her morning all mapped out and was making good timing until Synovi woke up with plans of his own. Her hair appointment was scheduled for ten, with her nail and pedicure appointment at two. She could easily reschedule with her nail tech, but Torin was about ready to hit Moo with a "Hey, girl!" text.

"Mmm." Torin moaned softly, her spine curling as Synovi pumped into her from behind.

For *that* dick, *his* dick, she'd shuffle her entire day around.

Dick dizzy thoughts only Synovi Black could give her, but Torin welcomed them like the orgasm she was on the brink of. Her eyes fluttered, gazing at him through the bathroom mirror. She'd gotten up to shower, and he followed behind her like a lost puppy. She felt open and exposed with her right leg hiked on the counter filled with his and her belongings. Torin made his place her home.

"This pussy is too fucking good," Synovi grumbled,

voice thick with sleep. He met her gaze and slid his hand between her legs. His fingers strummed her clit, and Torin gasped. "Let me feel it, Love."

Her chest heaved, and stomach tightened. "I-I came twice already," she whined.

The explanation she gave meant nothing to Synovi.

"That's not enough. I'm not satisfied," he claimed, making her pussy cream and drip even more.

Fucking bossy and greedy. Her pussy complied, clearly knowing who was running shit. Torin's head dropped as he pulled out and pumped back inside her wet walls with force.

"Oh, my gooo—"

His hand clamped around her mouth before her shout could be fully released. Synovi kissed her back and shoulder as he leaned forward to whisper in her ear. Further, planting his dick in the spot that had her losing it in the first place.

"Why you getting loud, huh? You want them to hear how good I'm fucking you?"

Her head shook as she groaned no against his palm; his smoldering gaze held her in place. Torin didn't know how he expected her to be silent when he was fucking her like this. It was an absurd question to ask.

"Be quiet then, and throw that ass back."

His request, more like a demand, was said with a smack to her ass. The hand around her mouth slid to her throat, and Synovi squeezed. Torin's eyes rolled as their skin clapped. Her yelling was kept to a minimum as she bounced her ass on him like she was on a pogo stick. The view... fucking ridiculous. Synovi knew exactly where he wanted her to get his name tatted. Her caramel ass smacking against his black-ink-coated midsection would play on a loop in his mind for the remainder of the day.

"I'ma nut," Synovi announced, breathing harshly, squeezing her narrow waist. Torin slow rolled it, contracting her muscles around him. "Fuck!"

"Who needs to be quiet now?" she taunted with a grin and moaned while gripping an ass cheek. "Let me feel your looove."

Torin had no problem requesting what she wanted, too, and he'd oblige, giving it to her any and every way she wanted it. Whenever. However. Truthfully, she didn't even have to ask. Synovi's face contorted as if he were in pain, but he was experiencing everything but that. With the sexiest grunt, he capitulated to her demands, releasing his seeds with an appreciative groan. Freakily, Torin grinned, face already shining with an afterglow, and tightened her grip around him. She wanted every drop.

"You... you so fucking nasty with your fine ass." Synovi huffed, slowly pulling out.

His compliment made her want to go another round. Spreading her cheeks, he looked on with pure lust and a hint of arrogance as his nut dripped from her swollen lips. Just as nasty and in love as she was, Synovi smeared their mess with the tip of his sensitive dick, toying with her clit in the process.

"Ooh, damn. Okay, Novi," Torin whimpered. "T-That's enough."

He patted her pussy with his now softening tool and

kissed her cheek before helping her down. "It's never enough. Come shower."

Twenty-seven minutes later, Torin stood at her side of the sink, oiling her body down. She wanted to crawl right back into bed after being so thoroughly dicked down, but there was business to handle.

"What?" she questioned, catching him staring.

Synovi stopped flossing and licked his lips. "That's that new oil you were telling me about?"

"Mhm. Been using it for like a month. You like it?"

"Yeah. Shit smells good," he said, picking the cylinder pump bottle up to read the label. "Luv Mi'Nex." He read the brand name aloud and nodded. "Creative name. She got stuff for men?" He asked, grabbing his deodorant to put on.

He finished and walked out of the bathroom, smacking her ass on his departure. Torin watched him the entire time, looking like she wanted to get another round in.

"Yes. I'll order you some." She blushed.

The cocoa butter and cashmere collection had been a favorite of hers since she started using it. It was the perfect musky yet warm, subtle scent for the fall. One thing about Torin, if she liked a product, she would spend her money on it. Especially if the product was from a Black-owned business.

"What time is your appointment?" Synovi asked, sliding a tank top on.

"Ten, but I'ma be late fooling with you."

He smirked. "You could always just wear your hair like that out of town."

"Boy, please." Torin sucked her teeth. "Do you see how quickly my hair shrank, and I didn't even get it wet?"

Synovi eyed the crinkly ball of hair atop her head. He had to admit, it was much bigger before they showered. Humidity caused it to shrink, and Torin knew it wouldn't stand a chance in Jamaica. She and the girls were flying out in a few days for Mia's birthday, and she couldn't wait to be around some water and just relax. The last couple of months had tried her like no other, and the trip would be just what she needed.

"Whatever you say, Love. What we gon' do while you gone?"

Torin chuckled, sliding her gray leggings on. "What y'all have been doing? Nothing's going to change in a week, babe."

"Shit, it might. Aye. You wearing a long shirt over those?"

Torin looked down at her legs. "My leggings?"

"Yeah. Your ass, man," he stressed, shaking his head. "That mothafucka is too fat in them."

"Novi." She cackled. "Please, okay. I can't help what my mama gave me."

"Nah, I know that, but damn. Make a nigga wanna go with you everywhere to conceal it," he joked, chuckling.

"I think gray leggings are to men what gray sweatpants are to us."

"What's that?" Synovi feigned ignorant.

Torin popped a hand on her hip. "A distraction. But normal people aren't going around staring at dick prints of all the men wearing gray sweats."

"So, I'm good to throw some on and run some errands?"

Torin nodded. "Mhm. As long as you put that dick up."

Synovi snorted a laugh. "You acting like this mothafucka detachable."

"I wish it was." She laughed. "I'd take it with me everywhere."

"Man," Synovi heaved, amused by her antics. "Shut yo' ass up."

Torin shrugged. She meant what she said. Being without him for a week was going to be torture, and she knew it. Not just without him but the girls as well. Like she knew she would, Torin loved them without question. It was hard not to, especially when they were the sweetest girls. Their parents may not have been worth shit but thank goodness their offspring weren't completely affected.

Torin and Synovi's daily routine changed and revolved around them. Like, sneakily fucking in the bathroom so that they couldn't hear. Or filling the fridges at their homes with food they both enjoyed. Even down to making Simone fully aware that Torin would sometimes be picking them up. They were a unit and moved as one, fitting Skylar and Kalie into the mix.

"Have they told you what they wanted to be for Halloween?" Synovi asked, spritzing some cologne on.

"Nope. Not yet. I'll probably dress up with them."

Synovi nodded. "Yeah, me too."

Her face lit up. "Awww, really? I'm sure they'd love that."

They would, and that was why he was doing it. Little things. They mattered the most. Synovi was creating memories with his family.

"Yeah. Gon' have to set some candy out and shit. Stuff I never got to do as a kid."

His words tugged at Torin's heart. "What's something else you didn't get to do as a kid but wanted to?"

Pondering, Synovi quieted for a beat. He'd seen so much on TV or read about in books. Experiences in life he thought he'd never get to partake in.

"It was a lot of shit, for real. Play Pop Warner Football and AAU basketball. Have my pops teach me how to change a tire. Get picked up early from school just because. Donuts with Dad. Shit I wanted but couldn't 'cause it was out of my control."

Torin walked over to him. Her thumb brushed across his bushy brow. "How about this? Make a list of things you wanted to do that you can control now, and we'll do them."

He smirked. "I like that idea. I ever tell you how attractively smart you are?"

"Mhm, but you can tell me again." She giggled.

Synovi squeezed her hip, and she kissed the tattoo on his sharp hairline.

"I love you."

"I love you more, baby. Now, come on before GiGi comes up here looking for us. I was supposed to be gone by now."

Finally dressed for the day, the duo made their way downstairs. Before they reached the last step, Torin gently reminded him to do something he'd been putting off all month.

"Don't forget to go visit your mama."

"A'ight," he muttered.

Torin knew he was a man of action, so she'd wait to hear how the visit went. She'd keep reminding him until then, though. Letting a situation linger for too long wasn't a good thing.

Racquel sitting on the couch with GiGi and Kalie surprised them both. Not because they didn't know she was in town but because she didn't tell them she was stopping by.

"Look at TorNovi finally gracing us with their beautiful presence," Racquel teased. "Good morning, y'all."

Torin playfully rolled her eyes. "Good morning. You and this nickname. Hang it up, buttercup."

She snickered. "Nope."

"Mornin' sis. You out early," Synovi noted.

"I told GiGi I'd be by to see her and check on KK this morning." She looked over her sister's outfit and smirked. "You look cute and comfy. Where you going?"

"Thank you. I have a hair appointment," Torin said, then giggled as she glanced at Kalie.

They'd come up with the nickname KK instead of baby girl, and it stuck. Having been running a fever the night before, GiGi offered to spend the night and look after her since they had a busy day today. By the looks of it, little Miss Thang was feeling just fine now.

"Somebody is feeling better," Synovi acknowledged. "Why you got her drinking coffee?"

"This baby can have some coffee. Now, hell. Don't start with us early this morning," GiGi fussed.

Kalie casually sipped from the Lilo & Stitch mug she made Torin buy while in TJ Maxx the other day. Having your first cup of coffee with your grandparents is like a Black birthright. Torin's grandpa was the first to give her a sip, and she was addicted up until her last year in college.

"She likes it too." Racquel laughed. "It's good, KK?"

"Mhm." She hummed. "Do you want some?"

Torin gasped, holding her chest. "Oh my gosh."

Synovi grinned big.

"What? Why y'all looking like that?" Racquel questioned, confused.

"Because," Torin mumbled on the verge of tears. "She hasn't said much of anything since she's been here."

GiGi pursed her lips. "All she needed was a lil' caffeine. Ain't that right?"

Kalie giggled, resting her head on GiGi's arm.

"I told y'all she'd warm up. She's been talking since I got here," Racquel informed.

Torin looked at Synovi, and he already knew what was on her mind. She wanted to celebrate the milestone. It wouldn't be her if they didn't. Wanting to make her a cup of tea before she headed out, Torin walked toward the kitchen but stopped in her tracks. A familiar fragrance invaded her nose, making her squint her eyes.

"I know you didn't use my perfume when you picked your package up earlier," Torin scolded.

Racquel frowned. "Torin, please don't start. I'm just home trying to enjoy my fall break."

"Then what is that that smells like it?"

Like a little sister who lived out of state but had an expensive shopping habit, Racquel got most of her packages sent to Torin's home. Her most recent purchase had been delivered and left on the porch the evening before, and she picked it up on her way to Synovi's crib.

"Oh. You're probably talking about this." Racquel picked up the pink tissue on the table and handed it to her.

"She sent the book wrapped in this?" Torin asked.

"Yes. It smells good as hell, too. It reminds me of the perfume from Zara. What brand is this, though? Because I'm about to buy some right now."

Torin happily sniffed the paper again and exhaled. "The one from Zara is a nice dupe. This smells like the Arabian one I told you about *months* ago. You don't be listening to me."

Racquel giggled. "I do. I forget some stuff if it's not pertained to school."

"Mhm. I bet. I know that's right, though. She's giving y'all an experience while unwrapping. I love that. Makes me want to step up my packaging for my spices."

She picked the book up from the coffee table and eyed the bold cover. It reminded her of a cover of an R&B album with a gritty undertone. The title intrigued her, too, and Torin wondered if the contents inside matched its vibe. She made a mental reminder to download it to her Kindle for her plane ride.

"Okay, y'all," she said, ten minutes later, with her thermo bottle of Nip's Tea in her hand. "I'm gone."

Synovi walked her way. He was heading out to work.

"Call us if y'all need anything," he said. "Racquel, don't be in here eating up all the snacks."

She waved them off. Her visit wasn't going to be long anyway. Khysen wanted to take her to brunch once he woke up, so she was killing time. He worked the overnight shift and needed a few hours of sleep before they kicked it.

"We won't be calling for anything," GiGi said. "See y'all later."

"See y'all later," Kalie repeated softly, waving bye.

Torin poked her lip out. "Ugh! My heart. I don't want to leave now," she whined.

Shaking his head, Synovi pulled the door to the garage open. "Come on. You already late."

"I know, I know."

Synovi held the driver's door open to her car, and she climbed inside. He leaned in once she buckled her seat-belt and gave her a kiss.

"I'll see you later. Have a good day, a'ight."

"Okay." She blushed, stomach fluttering. "I still have your card."

"I know." He chuckled. "Leave it when you go out of town."

Torin nodded. "Of course. Are you still going out with D'Marco nem later on?"

"Probably. We'll see. I gotta grab Sky from school and do a walkthrough of the building I told you about."

"Damn. That was quick. Boss found one already?"

"Yup. I'm ready to expand, but I'm not gon' rush into it."

His business was growing beyond his wildest

dreams, and the more his staff grew, the more space he needed. It was a blessing.

"As you shouldn't. I'll pick Skylar up. I should be done with my nail appointment by then."

"A'ight. Thank you."

"No need to thank me." She grinned. "We're a team."

Synovi smirked. "One that shows their appreciation."

"Oh. You did that this morning, but I'll listen again," she said, making them laugh.

"Yeah, I bet you will. See you later. I love you," he expressed effortlessly.

"Always?"

"In all ways. You know that."

She most definitely did.

"I love you, too."

"That's your last head for the day?" Torin asked Leighton over FaceTime.

"Yeah. I was supposed to be doing some starter locs, but they rescheduled," she answered. "Where you about to go?"

She had just left Moo's shop and was pulling up to Boss's office.

"I just pulled up to get this paperwork Synovi needs. Oh," she chirped. "I didn't know he was bringing them to the car."

"Who?"

"Boss. Hold on right quick," Torin said as she let the window down.

Boss strolled to the car, looking every bit of his name. He walked like he owned the place—more than a few places. He'd forgotten to give Synovi a few documents that couldn't be signed electronically.

"What's up? 'Preciate you for coming through last minute. He'll need these," he said, leaning down to pass a folder to her.

"No problem. Thankfully, you were in the area."

"Yeah. That's him on the phone?" Boss asked, nodding toward her cell that was propped up.

Torin swiveled it so he could see better. "No. This is my best friend."

That got Leighton's attention. She took in as much of Bostyn as she could and smirked, liking what she saw. A fine, Black ass man with a gorgeous smile and an even more beautiful Onyx complexion was just her type.

"How you doing?" Boss questioned smoothly.

"Much better now that you asked," Leighton flirted without shame.

"I should ask more often then."

Leighton chuckled. "You *could*, but am I going to let you is the question?"

"There should be no question about it," Boss replied easily.

The two were making Torin feel as if she were invading their conversation. Leighton had every intention of responding to him until Boss received a phone call. He pulled his phone from his pocket, gave Torin's screen a wink, and tapped the car's hood with his knuckle.

"I gotta catch this call. Drive safely," he said.

Torin let him know she would and pulled out of the lot.

"Girl," Leighton hissed lowly. "Who is he, and where did he come from?"

"I told you about him so long ago," Torin stressed. "That's Synovi's business partner. The one who got him started on commercial buildings."

Leighton smacked her lips. "You didn't tell me he looked like *that*. The fuck? Nigga winking at me like that... he don't even know."

Torin cackled. "He don't know what?"

"I can wink, too."

It quieted for two seconds before Torin busted out laughing, catching on to what she was saying. "Please get the hell off my phone!"

"I'm just saying. For real, though. What do you know about him? I could do my research, but I'd rather you tell me."

"I don't know much at all, honestly. He and Synovi aren't necessarily friends. More like close business associates. He owns a lot of properties around the city and out of state."

Leighton nodded. "Hmm. Okay, okay. I can see that. We gon' have to set up a cute double date."

"Let the man ask how your day was without getting irritated, and we can." Torin laughed.

Rolling her eyes, Leighton almost hung up. Her patience was tissue paper thin with men these days.

Especially with the ones who wanted to text her all day, asking what she was doing, how her day was, and when they could link up. She didn't have time for that shit, and unbeknownst to her, Boss didn't either.

"Whatever. You see I didn't get annoyed when he asked," Leighton said.

Torin smirked. "True. I'm glad you're working on being nicer."

"Whatever, hoe. Are you done packing?"

"For the most part, yes. I have a few more things to pick up, but that's it. I'm picking up Sky from school now, and we'll probably hit a few stores."

Leighton smiled. "Look at you being a good girlfriend and big sister."

"I do my best." Torin chuckled but meant it.

It had been an adjustment with Synovi having the girls throughout the week, but not as bad as they thought it'd be. Torin's schedule was set days in advance, so she had no problem stepping in where she could. Where Synovi wanted her to.

"You're doing an amazing job, friend. For real. You make me want to be a better woman if I meet a man with kids and decide to help him. Shit is going to take a miracle, but I know it can be done, thanks to you."

Torin laughed. "The fact that you're serious and kept a straight face is crazy. But thank you. I love those little girls already."

"I know you do. Let me finish this head and call you later on."

Torin told her okay as she pulled up to the school. Going to her texts, she sent one to Skylar, letting her know she was outside. Knowing she'd stay after school some days, Synovi bought Skylar a cell phone the first week they lived with him. Her iPad was a good way to keep in touch, but he needed her to have something else since she couldn't take it to school with her.

Three minutes later, Skylar came to the car. They no longer lived in the district Jade had them in, but thankfully, Simone lived in the area. They used her address for school, which wasn't a complete lie. They'd be staying with her some days and every other weekend.

"Hey! I thought my brother was picking me up," Skylar said, climbing in the backseat.

"Hey. He had a few meetings to go to, so he asked me to get you. Is that okay with you?"

Torin was looking at her through the rearview mirror but turned in her seat to face her when Skylar shrugged. It was done in a dejected manner that put her on alert.

"What's the matter, Sky?"

"Nothing," she grumbled.

"It can't be nothing. Did something happen at school that you wanna talk about?"

Skylar sniffled and wiped at her face. Torin had never seen tears fall so quickly. She was quiet until Skylar was ready to talk.

"Everyone in my class was talking about what they're going to get from the book fair tomorrow, and I got mad," she revealed.

"Okay. Was there a reason you got mad? I've heard you talking about the book fair all week."

"Because my mommy and daddy used to give me

money for it, but... but now they're not here, so I'm not going." She cried.

Torin unbuckled her seatbelt, opened her door, and pulled Skylar's door open in seconds. She hugged her as she cried and rubbed her back. This was the part of her relationship that broke her heart. Skylar was hurting, grieving in a way that Torin couldn't relate to but felt deeply.

"I just miss them," Skylar said once she pulled away.

"And it's okay to miss them. They'll always be with you in your heart and your memories."

Skylar nodded. "Okay."

Torin didn't know if she was overstepping with her next question, but she had to ask.

"Do you want to talk to someone about them and how you're feeling?" she questioned.

Sniffling, Skylar asked, "Someone like you?"

"You can always talk to me, but a professional. Someone like a counselor. They help you understand your feelings better and talk about your problems."

"I guess I could. I try talking to Kalie, but she's just a baby."

Torin's lip poked out. "Awww, Sky. I'm sure she listens to you."

Skylar chuckled lowly. "She does sometimes."

"Most little sisters do." She chuckled. "I'll check into some counselors, but in the meantime, you think about changing your mind for the book fair. If you don't want to go, you don't have to, but always know you can ask us for anything. We're not your mommy or daddy, but we have money for a book fair, okay?"

She nodded. “Okay. Thank you,” she said politely.

“You’re welcome. We good to go, or do you want to get some more talking and tears out first?”

“I’m okay. Can we go and get ice cream? You do have money for that, right?”

Torin laughed. “Yes, I do. And ice cream sounds good. We can do that.”

“Yay! Should we get my brother and Kalie?”

“Nope. Today is your day, and we’re doing what Sky wants.”

That put a smile on her face. Torin’s heart would disappear if these little girls melted it some more.

“Does that mean I get to sit in the front seat?” she questioned with a mischievous grin.

“No, that does not.” Torin laughed and closed her door.

Inhaling, she exhaled all of her worries and closed her eyes for a brief second. Leighton’s words about being a good girlfriend echoed through her mind, and she needed them more than ever. She thought a counselor would be perfect for Skylar, especially with all the transitions she was going through as a young lady. She made a mental reminder to bring it up to Synovi and hoped he thought about it. For right now, though, they were headed to get ice cream.

Seeing Unique being escorted inside the visiting room by guards would never be an image Synovi enjoyed.

At least she looks happy to see me, though, he thought as she approached the table he was sitting at. Synovi stood to his feet. This visit would be much different from the others, and he wasn't sure what to expect. They hugged quickly and took their seats.

"Well, look who it is." Unique beamed. "I'm so happy you came to see me."

Synovi grinned. "Me too. You lookin' good."

Her hair was flat ironed and pulled into a long ponytail. She'd also picked up some weight, but it looked good on her. The dullness he used to see in her eyes no longer lingered, and Synovi was hoping he wouldn't be the one to make it resurface.

"Thank you! So, what's been going on? I feel like we haven't talked in a minute," Unique expressed.

They hadn't, and Synovi felt kind of bad, but he was protecting her. There were only so many phone calls from her that he could avoid before she began to think something was wrong between them. Synovi had chickened out long enough not to tell her what was going on, and as a man, as her son, he felt the need to tell her face to face.

"Yeah, it does seem like that," he agreed, clearing his throat.

"Did I do something wrong?"

He squeezed his eyes shut at the hurt and confusion in her tone.

"Nah, nah. You didn't do anything. I just been going

through some shit and didn't want to involve you, but I need to."

"Oh. Well, okay. You know I can't do much from in here." She chuckled. "But tell me what's going on, and I'll try my best to help out."

Synovi swallowed his anxiety down as best as he could and eased her into the heartbreak.

"I hope we can still have a relationship after I tell you this."

"Why wouldn't we have one? What's going on?"

Her nerves were shot. Synovi's eyes filled with uncertainty.

"A'ight... so, look. Jade passed away some months back, and she put me in her will to become the guardian of her two little girls in the event that she dies. I don't know why she did it. Maybe out of spite or what, but that's why I haven't been answering your calls and keeping them short when we do speak."

Unique's body tensed, and her once bright smile dropped.

"I'm sorry, what?" Her voice shook, and her eyes blinked rapidly.

"The woman I was sleeping—"

"I heard you," she said, abruptly stopping him. "Just... give me... I need a second."

Synovi nodded, choosing not to speak until she did. Unique stood from the table, closed her eyes, stretched, and sat back down. When she sat back down and opened them, they glistened with such raw emotion that a sharp pain shot through Synovi's chest. He coughed loudly, covering his face in the fold of his elbow.

"You couldn't tell me this over the phone?" she wanted to know.

"No."

His answer was firm. Unique nodded her head.

"Okay. So, what'd you decide to do?" she asked, and it pained her to do so.

"I, uh. I have them. They been living with me for almost a month now."

She blew out a breath and leaned back in her chair. "Wow." She chuckled. "I can't believe this."

"They're my sisters," Synovi said in a defensive manner.

"I know that."

"So, what was I supposed to do? I couldn't just leave them."

He wanted her validation. Something he never received from her. Unique sat up and stared him in those gorgeous, inky eyes that told a story of the most broken, beautifully told story.

"You did what I know you'd do, and that's make sure those girls grow up in a loving, supportive home. Something I couldn't give you."

Unique wanted to cry, but she held it together. This wasn't a time to project her feelings; her son needed her.

"You did your best, too," Synovi said.

"And sometimes, your best isn't enough."

He had nothing to say to that, so he moved the conversation along.

"I just wanted to tell you before you caught wind from someone else. Shits a touchy subject, but you're not gonna be in here forever, and they're going to be in my life. I'd like it if you were in it, too, but I understand if that's asking for too much now."

"As of right now, in the moment, absolutely." Unique exhaled. "I wasn't expecting that at all. She just died like that?"

Synovi didn't mean to laugh, but her question caught him off guard. "From suffocation and alcohol poisoning," he revealed.

"Whew. God doesn't like ugly. He got them both on up out of here quick."

"Aye." Synovi choked on a laugh. "Let's change the subject."

Unique shrugged. "Fine with me. So, do you like being a big brother?"

He smiled proudly. "Yeah. It's a crazy feeling 'cause I never had siblings, but I love it."

"You know what's crazy? You used to boss your little cousins and kids around like they were your kids, and you were the youngest." Unique chuckled. "I guess you were always meant to be a big brother."

"I guess so. I know it's too soon, but I hope this doesn't change anything between us."

Reassurance. He needed it from her like his next breath. Her answer would show him if their relationship had truly grown or if it was all a front. Synovi hoped things didn't change between them because he'd finally reached a point in his life where he wanted Unique in it forever, regardless of her being behind bars.

"Of course not. You're *my* son. Nothing or no one will ever stop me from having a relationship with you. Isn't that why I'm in here?" She tipped her head to the side, waiting for his answer.

Synovi chuckled lowly. "You got a point."

He could live with that answer. There was so much more he wanted to tell her, but the wounds were still fresh. To his surprise, Claudia, Omar's mama, had reached out to Simone asking if she and her daughter could meet the girls on Thanksgiving. Simone was okay with it but wasn't sure how Synovi would feel, so she told her she'd get back with her after they discussed it.

Synovi was still indecisive. A part of him knew how important family was, but so was his sisters' upbringing. Too much foul shit had gone on with them in the mix, and he wasn't trying to subject them to anymore if he didn't have to. He and Torin planned to spend the day at Tracee's anyway, and that was an entirely different family that he'd have to take into consideration.

Being able to make decisions for the betterment of his and their future was a privilege, something he wasn't given back then. If he had any say so, Synovi would keep acting like anything connected to Omar or Jade didn't exist. For now, they didn't. When they got of age, he'd let Skylar and Kalie decide whether they wanted them in their lives.

eleven

"Oh, my gosh." Skylar groaned with laughter. "You're doing them wrong. Here, let me do it."

Synovi eyed Kalie's lightly swirled baby hairs he'd worked hard on. "I think they look good, KK."

"Let's show Torin," Kalie said, as if his approval wasn't satisfactory.

Grabbing his phone off the counter, Synovi called Torin on FaceTime. Being a big brother who took his role seriously was endearing and comical all at once. He'd taken thirty minutes to put two ponytails in her head and was trying to lay her edges without Skylar's assistance. Big sister was to the rescue before he gave Kalie a headache.

"Hey, baby. What's up?" Torin grinned, answering her phone.

He panned the camera on Skylar fixing up her sister's edges. "They got me in here breaking a sweat."

"No, we don't!" Skylar giggled. "He just needs a little bit more practice."

"They didn't have enough squiggle," Kalie said, making Torin laugh.

Synovi shook his head. "Man, her hair thick as hell. I hooked her ponytails up, though."

Torin examined them as he showed off his skills. Kalie's part was slightly crooked, but that didn't matter.

"Okay! I see you putting your skills to work. They look good and moisturized. If you'd let her get some braids or little twists, you wouldn't have gone through all of that."

"Nah. She's good," he said, kissing Kalie's cheek. "We got it handled. When you coming home, though?"

Laughing, Torin shook her head. She and Mia flew out of town to handle the final touches for her spices and would be home in the morning. Synovi was acting as if she'd been gone a week like her previous trip. He wasn't the only one, though.

"Right! Because we're tired of eating noodles," Skylar blurted.

"Really, Sky? I ain't fed y'all no real food?" Synovi asked in disbelief. "Just gon' throw me under the bus."

Kalie cracked up laughing while Skylar giggled. "I like noodles, brother."

"Thank you, KK," he exaggerated. "I be hooking them shits up. Sky hating."

"Am not. I just miss her cooking," she expressed.

That warmed Torin's heart. She missed them and couldn't wait to hop on her flight in the morning.

"I'll be home tomorrow, Skylar. You know, you could've called my mama or had GiGi come over. What'd y'all eat for breakfast?"

"Wasn't no need for all that. I made them pancakes, bacon, and eggs," Synovi answered.

"It was good," Kalie said.

She was the pickier eater of the bunch and only ate the pancakes and an orange, but that was fine with Synovi. As long as she was fed, he was good.

"Check you out. I'ma have to add you to my team," Torin joked.

"Yeah, you do that. Y'all good out there?"

Torin nodded, moving around her hotel room. They were getting ready for their last meeting and then heading to dinner.

"Yes. Everything is aligned and ready to go. Just... keeping my patience on the backend."

"That's all you can do. We're proud of you," Synovi said.

"So proud, girl," Skylar added.

"A'ight. It's time to go. Go put y'all shoes and jackets on."

He lifted Kalie from the sink, and they ran into the living room. He had a full day planned for them, and they didn't even know it yet.

"Where y'all going?" Torin asked, stepping inside the bathroom. She propped the phone on the counter, and Synovi forgot what she asked him.

"Damn," he expressed, licking his lips. "Yo' titties look good in that lace bra, Love."

She blushed hard. "Thank you."

"Lemme see something right quick."

"Baby, no." She laughed. "You need to finish getting the girls ready."

"They can wait. Just pull your pants down. I know you got the matching panties on."

She did. Unfastening her suit pants, catering to his requests, Torin lowered them. She didn't have to be told to turn around, knowing he wanted a view of her fat ass.

"Mm. Make a nigga wanna catch a flight to you," he spoke lustfully and grinned. "Send me some pictures."

"Oh. I was going to do that anyway. You called first and messed up the plan."

They shared a laugh as he stepped into the living room.

"I had to show you my hard work. KK, don't forget *your* iPad. We not doing all that whining and shit today."

"Stop cursing at her," Torin fussed.

"My bad. Sorry, I'ma stop using bad words at you, okay?"

Kalie pinched his lips. "Good."

"That's right! Get him." Torin snickered. "Now, where y'all going? You never told me."

"I got distracted. We going to do some community service at Solace Place and then hitting the malls and stuff."

"Awww. Y'all doing all of that without me. Y'all couldn't wait until tomorrow?"

"Nah, 'cause I don't need three of y'all breaking my pockets." He chuckled. "We can run it back, though. You know the holidays coming up."

The trio headed toward the garage, and Synovi helped Kalie into the backseat as Skylar climbed in on the other side. Kalie dug around in her fuzzy, heart-shaped purse and looked up at him with a panicked expression.

"What's the matter?" Synovi asked.

Her bottom lip poked out. "My lip gloss."

"You know where it's at?"

"No! She always losing it," Skylar blurted.

"Shut up!"

"Oop. I know that's not KK talking like that," Torin said, stunned.

Saying shut up as a kid, at least in Torin's home, was like cursing. Her mama didn't play that, and she wasn't either.

"Aye. Don't use that word. Say, be quiet," Synovi said.

"But she does need to be quiet. I don't lose it," Kalie whined, on the verge of tears.

Synovi exhaled and shook his head. He didn't have time for her to go searching for it. All of this estrogen floating around had him wanting a strong drink, and he wasn't a drinker. As soon as they went to sleep tonight, he was rolling up.

"Check the second drawer on the left soon as you walk in the kitchen. It should be an extra one in there," Torin said.

"I'll be right back," he told them, walking back inside the house.

Going to the drawer as she'd instructed, Synovi opened it and grabbed the clear tube filled with pink gloss. Thankfully, he hadn't set the alarm yet and did on his way out.

"This it?" he asked, handing it to Kalie.

"Yes! Thank you, Torin." She beamed.

"You're welcome, my girl. Make sure you don't

misplace this one, or we'll have to wait until next month to order some more," she said.

One of her friend's daughters started their lip gloss line, and Torin had to support her. She let the girls pick their own set and had them waiting when she picked them up from school one day. How Kalie was only down to one tube from the Good Girl Bloss set was beyond her.

Synovi closed her door, headed to his side, and hopped in. "That's the only kind she likes?"

"For now." Torin laughed. "I hope y'all have a good time today. Send me pictures. Don't be stingy like they can only hang with you."

Synovi smirked and panned the camera on them in the backseat. Their iPads had their undivided attention for now.

"You jealous?" he jested.

"Nope. Just remember that when we go do something without you."

Laughing, Synovi backed out of the garage. "Yeah, yeah. Call us later."

"I will. Love y'all," she said.

"We love you, too!" Skylar shouted. "Bring me a gift back with you, please."

Torin giggled. "Sure thing."

"A'ight, Love."

They hung up and headed to their first destination. Synovi thought about how he could break it down to them, including how and when he became their brother, without revealing all the tragedy in between. It made perfect sense to show them a glimpse of where he'd grown up—a place he once considered home. Letting them do a little community service with Mrs. Cannon and the culinary staff wouldn't hurt either.

It took perseverance, prayer, and a lot of discipline to get to where he was today, and he wanted to show them that, no matter what, you had to keep going. A text came through from Torin as soon as he made it to the end of the second block.

> Don't forget to ask the outreach advocate about counselors for Skylar.

Synovi rolled his tongue over his teeth. He was grateful for the reminder but dreaded doing so. Normally, he'd ask Ms. Reid for referrals, but she was on maternity leave and he didn't want to bother her. She wouldn't have seen it as a bother, but still. Synovi was being considerate. Like she said she would, Torin brought up the idea to him after her talk with Skylar that day.

He wasn't against it but wanted Skylar to be the one to agree to see someone. As a young girl going through so many transitions, talking about them with someone was something Synovi and Torin wished they had. So, if the resources were available and Skylar agreed, Synovi was signing her up.

"Where'd you say we were going again?" Skylar asked.

"To where I used to live before y'all moved with me."

She stared out the window. "My mama said she couldn't wait for us to all be together."

Synovi drew his head back. Her unexpected comment

threw him way off, but he kept his composure. It wasn't the first time Skylar brought Jade up, and it wouldn't be the last.

"Like me, her, and y'all?" he questioned.

Skylar shrugged. "I don't know. I guess just us three here right now since she's gone."

The truck fell silent for a few seconds before Skylar continued. "I like living with you, though. It's not so bad."

"I like you living with me, too, Sky. You know I'd do anything for you and KK, right?"

He looked into the rearview mirror to catch her wet eyes on him. She nodded solemnly.

"Yes," she whispered.

"I mean that. I love y'all, and no matter what happened in the past or what anyone tells you about me, remember that, okay?"

She nodded again and wiped a tear from her cheek. "Okay. I love you, too."

"I love you more!" KK squealed, not wanting to be left out.

Getting choked up, Synovi cleared his throat and focused on the road with blurred vision. It took him a while to accept his past and reality, but he had to. Otherwise, he'd be stagnant. For his family... Synovi wanted to be the best man he could be. He cherished the family he came from, but the one he chose to create was his number one priority now.

I had to step up and be a brother and father figure. Shit gets wicked when you don't have one, he thought.

He never wanted to be one of those people who refused to excel in life because it was hard. It was only going to get harder. But he had to trust that it got better, and it did, ten times over. Everything, no matter how they came about, had worked out in his favor.

twelve

If there was one thing working with Bostyn and building a brother-ship with him had taught Synovi, it was to live up to the meaning of being the boss. It wasn't about the amount of money you brought in, the car you drove, or how much power you presumably had.

It was about a person's character.

Their moral compass in a world full of envious, greedy, hateful individuals.

What made you, as the boss, stand out? Not just as the head person in charge but also your overall disposition. Behind that title, were you a decent human being? It was something Synovi asked himself and his employees before they were hired at SBCS. Being the boss didn't amount to shit if you had a bunch of workers with marbles for brains and a lazy work ethic.

Thankfully, his staff went hard for the brand, and that was why they were all sitting in the meeting room, full of elation.

"Yo!" one breathed out.

"I can get my kids the stuff on their Christmas list," a young father mumbled with tears in his eyes.

"Thank you, Jesus!" a woman praised.

A plethora of incoherent gratitude echoed around the room. Synovi stood back with a humble smile and his heart full. "As my appreciation and love for y'all and everything y'all do for SB, I just wanted to give y'all a bonus."

"But I just started working here two weeks ago," a young girl said in utter shock.

"You're still an employee, right?" Synovi asked.

Her head bobbed as she pressed the check to her chest. The extra money was just what she needed to help finish paying off her tuition.

"Thank you so much!" she said.

"You're welcome. Christmas is in a week, and we'll be closed from the twenty-third through the twenty-fifth. Meaning we won't be accepting any new cleaning requests, no matter who it is. If you're on schedule to work in between those days, thank you, and be safe. If you're off, enjoy this time with your loved ones. Get with Eboni before y'all leave to update any schedule changes before the new year. Merry Christmas!"

"Merry Christmas, boss man!" Tae shouted, hitting a jig.

Synovi chuckled and shook his head while pointing at him. "Stay out of trouble."

"Always! I'm finna hit the casino with my cousins and triple this shit."

As other employees murmured on about what they had planned and gathered their things to leave, Synovi headed to his office. He'd be working all week, making sure clients' homes were taken care of and doing some rush jobs in case people called in. He knew they would, especially with that money burning a hole in their pockets. Before he could do all that, he needed to check his email for a response he'd been waiting for.

Stepping inside his office, he smiled at the photo on his desk. Torin and the girls had gone to Office Max and got a picture of the four of them to put on his desk. Skylar tried convincing him the picture would look even better with a puppy in it, but Synovi wasn't going for that.

Pulling up his emails, he eyed the unread ones until he came across the one he needed to see most. Opening it, his eyes quickly scanned the contents of it, and he sat back in his chair. Thunderous claps resounded throughout the space, giving way to his achievement. Another one he hadn't expected to ever be presented to him. But being in the right place at the right time was something.

"I'm not staying late today," he said to himself, drafting a response after downloading the PDF file.

"What you in here clapping about?" D'Marco said, entering.

"We just secured another contract, and right before the holidays. I'm hype."

D'Marco's head bobbed, and he started clapping. "Shit, that's something to celebrate. Congratulations, my boy."

"Thank you, thank you. You work this week?"

"Yeah. We going out of town Saturday morning, though."

Synovi nodded. "That's right. I forgot. I was gon' tell you to bring Nya by the crib. The girls been asking to see her."

D'Marco smiled at the thought of his daughter. "You know she had that little cold and shit. She's good now, though. We'll slide through later on."

"Bet. I'ma see if Torin wanna throw something on the grill, then. I'm leaving early," he said, already tasting her grilled salmon and ribs.

In the Midwest, if the temperature was at least fifty degrees, the grill was lit up. For it to almost be January and the city still receiving warmer than usual days, was crazy, but they weren't complaining.

"A'ight bet. Let me see what time Nikki gets off, and we'll be through there."

The friends slapped hands, and Synovi shut his computer down for the day forty minutes later. He said bye to his lingering staff and Eboni before hopping in his truck. Dialing up Torin's number, he waited for her to answer. He had some good news beyond his to share with her, and it needed to be done in person.

"Hey, baby," she greeted upon answering.

"My Love," Synovi half-sang.

Torin laughed. "Oh. Okay. It's one of those days, huh?"

"Yes, indeed. Where you at? I need to tell you something. Can you get away for lunch?"

"I'm at the kitchen, and yes, I can. I have something to tell you, too. I'm just wrapping up a lunch delivery order."

Boss shit.

Taking the day off early to celebrate his wins and treat his lady. Synovi loved his life.

"A'ight. I'll be through there in twenty minutes. Which location you at?"

"The one on Chestnut," she replied.

He told her okay and headed in that direction. Even though Synovi had bought her a new commercial kitchen space at the end of last year, Torin still utilized her first one. Over the summer, she rented it out to aspiring chefs, party promoters and even held one-on-one cooking classes.

That was new to her list of things she provided, but she enjoyed it. Her millionaire client, Judah, hired her for a date night, since his woman was trying to up her skills in the kitchen. Torin found that so adorable that he'd catered to her love language in a way that meant the most to her.

When he pulled up to the kitchen seventeen minutes later, Synovi hopped out and made the short walk to the building. Upon entering, the strong smell of garlic, peppers, and an array of herbs and spices tingled his nose. His stomach growled, reminding him that he needed to eat.

"What's up? How y'all doing?" He spoke to a few of her employees as he walked through.

They were all dressed in custom Kaine's Kitchen chef wear. Synovi loved the uniform and made a mental reminder to get more cleaning shirts made for his staff. They greeted him with waves and head nods.

Spotting Torin at one of the double-oven gas stoves, he stepped her way. She couldn't hear him approach over the R&B music they had playing, but she felt him as soon as he was close enough. Synovi smirked, loving the view of her in her little culinary get-up. With black pants, a white chef's coat, and her hair net on, Torin still looked good.

Synovi hugged her around the waist and kissed her neck. "What's up, Love?"

She melted against his chest. "You got here fast. I know that's right. Do the dash about me." She giggled.

"Always. What you making?"

He stood beside her, eyeing the cream-colored icing in the bowl and strawberries next to it.

"Some strawberry cheesecake cookies. They're for an order, but I'ma make extra for the house."

"Damn. Those sound good. Make sure you dice the strawberries up small. You know KK hates the texture if not."

Torin snickered. "I know, baby. That's why they're macerating first. I'll use my hand blender to smash them afterward."

"They're doing what right now?" he questioned, eyeing the glass bowl of fruit again.

"Macerating. It means soaking food in a liquid to soften it, but in this case, I just sprinkled a bit of sugar on them. It draws out the juices so that they become soft and mushy... just like KK likes." She snickered.

Synovi nodded his head, loving how she easily taught him something new. He kissed her cheek. "That shit just made my dick hard," he whispered in her ear.

Torin squirmed out of his embrace and looked his way. "Don't start nothing while I'm on the clock, sir."

"You said you could get away for lunch. I think it's time we take that break."

Synovi licked his lips, and Torin's pussy thumped.

"*We*? You speak French now?" She smirked.

"I'm very fluent in amour. That's the only language I need to know."

Her eyes darted around the kitchen for someone to finish making the cookies. Spotting one of her top bakers, Torin waved her over.

"Hey, Mika. Can you finish these cookies for me? You've made them before, right?"

"Yes. Add some of the strawberries to the frosting?"

Torin nodded her head. "Mhm. And just pipe it on the cookies before sprinkling the graham crackers. I'll be right back."

"Gotcha," Mika said.

On the way to her office, she removed her gloves and hair net, tossed them in the trash, and washed her hands. Synovi followed behind her down the hall, playfully patting her ass cheeks along the way. He closed the door and locked it once they entered her office.

"Un, un." She giggled, hearing the click. "Don't be locking doors."

"Need my privacy with you. What's up, Love." He grinned as she leaned against her desk. "You should've dressed up in just an apron for me on Halloween."

Torin snickered. "I got you next year. Now, what is it you needed to tell me? It sounded urgent."

"You said you had to tell me something, too. Go first."

Torin smiled brightly. "The FDA approved my spices. I got the email—oh, my gosh!" she shrieked as

Synovi unexpectedly picked her up and swung her around.

"I'm so fucking proud of you," Synovi said, placing her on her feet.

"Thank you. I wasn't expecting them to send it before the holiday, but I'm glad they did. Now, I can fully enjoy them."

Even though he'd told her not to be anxious about the approval, Torin couldn't help it. She didn't have to anymore. Months from now, KAINES will be lining the grocery store shelves and people's seasoning cabinets and drawers.

"I'm glad they did, too. You relaxing for the rest of the month, though," he said.

"That's the plan." She sighed. "Now, your turn."

"I secured a contract with BLAKC to clean their property starting January first, and I got you an interview with them."

Torin's jaw dropped. "Wait. You can't just say that so nonchalantly like that." She laughed. "That's huge!"

"Man. Tell me about it."

BLAKC, the main radio station in Kansas City, had hired SBCS to clean for them. A brief run-in with Kent, one of the on-air personalities, at Quik Trip, had turned into another amazing opportunity. Which, in turn, gave Synovi a chance to put his boo on as well. Catering for their team and even being placed on the mic to promote her business would only help get the word out about KAINES quicker. Synovi couldn't wait to brag about his woman.

"Congratulations, baby, and thank you so much for

always speaking my name in rooms you're in. That means so much to me."

She meant everything to him, so it was only right he came hard behind her.

"You know it ain't nothing. You do the same for me. I wanna see us both win forever."

She nodded her head. "Absolutely. I guess we're just bouncing wins off each other, huh?"

"Yeah." He chuckled.

"Good, because I have one more thing to tell you."

Synovi's head cocked to the side. "You trying to one-up me?"

"Nooo." She laughed. "This has been in the making."

Going around to the drawer of her desk, Torin pulled out an envelope and handed it to him. She knew if she kept it at his or her home, the surprise would be ruined if it got lost or opened. Synovi gave her a mischievous smirk.

"What's in here?"

"Remember I asked you to write down some of the things you wanted to do as a kid but couldn't?" Synovi nodded his head. "Well, I figured we'd go ahead and start scratching things off. Open it up."

Slowly, Synovi unsealed the flap. His eyes shot up to hers when he pulled out custom-made tickets to Disney World. Torin had designed them herself, adding their names with a fake barcode to scan. He couldn't believe this.

"Nah." He chuckled. "You deadass bought us tickets to Disney World. Are you serious right now?"

The young, unloved, and forgotten about Synovi was jumping for joy right now. He'd forgotten all about sharing that list with her. Torin was a Godsend. She was mending wounds he thought would never fade. Amid the chaos and the unknown, she came through unexpectedly, changing the trajectory of Synovi's life for good. There was no way he was ever letting her go.

"I am. We leave on the twenty-third and get back on the twenty-sixth. Your office is closed those days, so..." She chuckled.

The perks of still having his schedule had worked in her favor.

"This is crazy," he said, taking a seat in one of the nearby chairs. With his emotions high, Synovi couldn't do anything but shake his head. "You really love a nigga, huh? Everything I come with."

"I do. I love those little girls you brought into my

world, too. They deserve this. *You* deserve this, baby. I hope you didn't have anything planned."

He shook his head. "I didn't. But I know you did. You didn't have any orders and families to cook for on Christmas?"

"Nope. I delegated those events to my staff if they wanted them. I want to be with my family for the holidays. I've catered to enough over the years. I think it's okay to go missing with mine for a few days," she said.

Standing, Synovi pulled her flush against his chest and kissed her lips. "Your family. Say that shit again."

"My family," she enunciated slowly and surely.

"That sounds good to a nigga, Love. Real talk. Thank you for this. The girls are going to lose it."

She laughed. "I already know they are. Oh! I invited D'Marco, Nya, and Nikki, too. So, they'll fly out with us that morning."

"That nigga didn't say anything about this when I just talked to him."

She laughed. "Um, he wasn't supposed to. It's called a surprise for a reason."

"You right. I gotta think of a way to out-surprise you," he said.

"I know what you can give me."

He humped her, making her feel his erection. "This dick?"

"No." Torin giggled. "I mean, yeah, but some food for right now. I'm starving, and you owe me lunch."

"I owe you more than that. But let's start there."

epilogue

FEBRUARY 2024

"Girl, if you yawn one more time in my ear," Leighton scolded playfully.

As if the word triggered her senses, Torin yawned again. She was so happy to be pulling into her driveway; her bed was screaming her name. Seeing Synovi's truck only made her that much more ready to get in the house.

"My bad. I'm so tired. I hate having to run errands after a long day. Especially during rush hour."

"Oh. That's the worst. You don't have to tell me. Have you made it home yet?"

She cut her ignition, shut the garage, and popped the trunk. "Yep. I just got here."

"Okay. Well, text or call me later."

Torin told her she would, and they hung up. Climbing out of the car, she strolled to the trunk and grabbed the bags of groceries and other things before heading inside. As soon as she stepped inside, her lavender-scented plug-ins could be smelled. Along with that scent was one of a home that had been and was getting thoroughly cleaned.

She entered the living room and spotted Skylar putting together a new puzzle while Kalie lay across the couch on her iPad. They'd made themselves right at home in her place, and she was grateful for that.

"Hey, girls," she spoke.

Kalie's head popped from behind the screen. "Hi, TorNovi!"

"KK, no." Racquel cracked up from her iPad. They were on FaceTime like homegirls, just chatting away.

Torin couldn't help but laugh. "Racquel has corrupted my sweet lil' baby."

"Tell me about it." Skylar huffed. "Where are you coming from?"

"The store, if you must know, Miss Nosey," Torin joked.

"I hope you're cooking today!" Skylar shouted at her back as Torin entered the kitchen.

She had them spoiled just as badly as Synovi did. Placing the bags on the table, Torin didn't bother to make a peep as she stood back, watching him clean. Not just a regular routine clean, but a deep one. Synovi had removed the knobs off the stove and soaked them. He washed the baseboards with scalding water with a few drops of peppermint oil and dusted every light fixture without a stepstool.

Torin was in heat!

Seeing her man be a man and clean her home was the most erotic visual ever. It was how he'd left her smitten when they first met, and nothing had changed; it only intensified. With the music going, he knew she probably thought he hadn't heard her, but he did. Synovi waited for her to walk by him with what she told him she was picking up at the store.

"It ain't gon' take itself, Love," he said, facing her with a smirk.

Torin sighed. "I know. Hi. It smells and looks good in here."

Synovi kissed her lips, staying there and squeezing her booty. "You smell good, too. How was your day?"

She yawned. "Long and probably about to be even longer."

"Cheer up." He chuckled, spanking her ass as she walked by him to the guest bathroom. "It ain't the end of the world if you are."

Torin didn't bother to reply. Closing the door, she removed the pregnancy test from the plastic bag and stared at it. Her cycle had always been irregular, but the bitch was acting straight-up ridiculous now. It'd been missing in action for far too long, and Synovi had peeped it. She didn't think she was pregnant, but guessing didn't deliver facts, so here she was. Just as she sat down to pee, Synovi knocked on the door.

"I haven't taken it yet," Torin called out.

"A'ight. I wanna be in there with you, though."

She snickered, ripping the package open. "Let me pee first, baby."

It quieted on the other end, and Torin handled her business. Placing the test on the thick napkin, she flushed and washed her hands before pulling the door open. Synovi was still there with a grin on his face.

"Can I come in now?"

"Yes," she said, stepping aside.

He closed the door and locked it behind him. It'd been a habit of his forever, and he was glad it stuck. Having two kids in the house who thought every space was theirs was crazy. And Skylar proved him right just as she padded into the kitchen and knocked.

"Yes?" Torin called out.

"Y'all okay in there?"

"We're just having a quick chat. We'll be out soon."

She was quiet for a beat. "Hmm. Okay."

"Don't stand by the door, Sky," Synovi said, knowing her all too well already. "Remember we talked about privacy and setting boundaries?"

"Fine." She huffed. "I know what she's taking anyway!" she yelled, scurrying back into the living room. Torin smirked while Synovi just shook his head. He'd already grown a few grays in his head since they'd moved with him, and more were sure to make an appearance.

"She can't help herself," Torin said.

"I know, but she gotta learn boundaries. We getting there. Now, back to you," he said, glancing at the screen of the test. His eyes widened, and Torin's stomach fell to her feet.

"What! What does it say?" she whispered in a hiss.

"Damn, Love." Synovi sighed, picking it up. "You're not pregnant."

When he grinned, she punched him in the arm. "You play too much!"

"I had to get you. Scary ass. Was nervous for no reason."

"As a Black woman, I have a million reasons to worry, even more when I'm pregnant. So, yes, I was nervous. I'm glad I'm not, though. Whew." She exhaled.

Synovi didn't take her words to heart. A baby right now would've added much more to their plates. Knowing ways to prevent pregnancy and utilizing the methods were different. How was she not supposed to freak on her man during ovulation week when that dick was so good, and it made her want to be chained to it? She wasn't sure, but they were gonna have to figure something out.

"Yeah, we got time for all that," he said, washing his hands. "I wanna put a ring on your finger first, anyway."

Torin blushed and looked down at her hand. "I'd like that."

"Yeah? Mrs. Torin Kaine-Black sounds sexy as fuck."

"Mrs. B, if you nasty," she said and winked, making him shake his head.

"Quit watching that lady, man. Ol' freaky ass." He laughed.

Torin rolled her eyes playfully. "Whatever. That name does have a ring to it. What're we going to do until then because I don't want another scare?"

He pulled her in between his legs as he leaned against the sink. "We can look into the healthiest options of birth control 'cause I know wearing a condom isn't what you want me to do."

"Hell no, it's not. We'll just be careful until I talk to my doctor."

Synovi rubbed her back, relaxing her even more. "Good. Until then, you gon' keep giving me this good shit between your legs and your love."

"I am?" she jested, squinting her eyes.

"Yeah. What, you wanna shake on it?"

Smirking, Torin pushed back some and stuck her hand out.

"It's a deal once we shake hands," she said.

"I know it is," Synovi replied, grabbing her hand. He shook it with a grin. "That's how we got in this predicament in the first place. I was never going to keep it professional with you, Love. Believe that."

Keep reading for bonus content.

bonus content

April 2024

"You like your hair?" Torin asked Kalie, who stared at herself in the floor-to-ceiling mirror inside Selyse's shop.

Slowly, Kalie shook her braided ponytails with clear and purple beads. Leaning into the mirror, she ran a finger over her finely swirled baby hair and smiled.

"Yes. It's so pretty and neat," she replied.

Torin smirked. "What do you know about something being neat?"

"These kids have been here before," Selyse said, smiling. "You did such a good job today, Kalie. I'll see you again next month."

"I have to ask my brother," Kalie said, making Torin shake her head with amusement.

While Skylar seemed to be attached to Torin's side, Kalie didn't let Synovi breathe if he was in her presence. Somehow, he convinced her to get her hair braided by one of the best braiders in the city, and the first-time experience wasn't that bad. She only winced and whined when she got it blow-dried.

"She didn't even want to come, and now she has to ask him." Torin laughed. "Whew. These girls and their brother."

Selyse smirked. "Trust me. I already know."

"Thank you so much, though. It'll save us so much time when getting ready."

"You're welcome. Thank you for trusting me with her hair."

Selyse had the Midas touch when it came to braiding, but styling kids' hair was her specialty. She made them comfortable, gently handling their hair as if it were hers. It was Selyse's nurturing aura and soothing voice as well. No matter how much the child cried or got upset, she remained calm, which was most important.

"We'll be back for sure. Come on, KK," Torin said, gathering her belongings.

Kalie looked up at Selyse, focusing on the beads around her waist. "Can I have one of those?"

"No, you cannot." Selyse grinned at her pouting. "But you can have one of these." She slid a beaded turquoise bracelet with gold charms off her wrist and handed it to her.

It hung loosely on Kalie's wrist, but she didn't care. She pushed it up her arm until it was secure. "Thank you! We're leaving now."

Selyse giggled. "Okay, girl. See you later."

"Thank you again," Torin said, following a skipping Kalie out the door.

Opening the back door to Synovi's truck, Torin

helped her in before climbing in the passenger seat. Synovi turned around in the driver's seat and smirked, seeing Kalie already making her way onto the middle console.

"You see my hair! It didn't even hurt," she said.

"Check you out, KK. You look so pretty," Synovi told her.

Blushing, Kalie's head lowered as she giggled. "Thank you! Look what else I got?"

"Oh, my gosh," Skylar groaned. "We're gonna be late to Auntie Simone's house."

"No, we not," Kalie fussed, whipping her head around. She smacked Skylar's leg, making her push her off the seat. "Owww!" Kalie wailed, fake crying.

They swatted hands at one another, fighting like only a little and big sister did. Especially when the youngest thought she was the boss.

"A'ight. Y'all need to chill out. KK, get up. Stop being dramatic and keep your hands to yourself. You too, Sky," Synovi said.

"She hit me first!" Skylar huffed, slamming her back into the seat. "That's why your hair is ugly."

"You ugly!" Kalie insulted, sticking her tongue out. "That's why I got a bracelet, and you don't."

"So, what little girl."

Synovi glanced at Torin, who was smirking and shook his head. She knew what he wanted her to do without even saying it.

"Hey," Torin said, facing them. "Both of y'all cut it out and apologize, or neither of y'all will be going to Simone's house."

Skylar sucked her teeth. "Sorry," she apologized first with a huff.

Kalie didn't mumble a word as she climbed off the floor.

"KK, you didn't hear me?"

She rolled her eyes, and it took everything in Torin not to laugh. Kalie had her days where she didn't talk to anyone but Skylar, and then there were days like today when she showed her true charismatic behavior.

Kalie crossed her legs and folded her arms with a pout. "I'm sorry, but not all the time."

Synovi busted out laughing, making the entire truck do the same. They let them speak their minds but stopped it when things got disrespectful. Raising his sisters was no walk in the park, but moments like these made the challenging days worth the sacrifices he made.

When they pulled up to Simone's house, the girls eagerly climbed out, running to the front door with their overnight bags dangling off their shoulders. Synovi followed behind them a minute later, carrying a few grocery bags. Even though it was her weekend to keep them, he still tried looking out for them in their absence. Simone didn't always have the snacks they liked, and they'd run through a jug of juice like it was no one's business.

"Hey, my babies." Simone greeted them with a smile and hugs.

"We not babies, TT," Kalie informed.

Simone's head cocked to the left. "What! Since when? You got your hair done all cute, and now you're a big girl?"

"Yes." Kalie nodded matter-of-factly, making Simone chuckle.

"Well, okay then, big girl. Come on in. Hey, Synovi. How are you?"

Synovi gave her a head nod. "What's up? I'm straight. Trying not to get any more gray hairs."

"I heard that. Oh, thanks for the groceries," she said, waving back at Torin, who waved from the truck.

"No problem. Don't forget about Sunday," he said just as Skylar rushed back their way. "What's wrong?"

"You're coming back to get us, right?"

Her question made his chest tighten, and distant memories flooded his brain. The same question was presented to Unique more than a few times when he was a kid until she never returned. She just stopped showing up one day, and that cemented Synovi's resentment toward her. Thankfully, they were able to cross the bridge that survived the burn of her and society's actions.

"Yes. I'll be here on Sunday to pick y'all up, or Simone will bring y'all to me," Synovi answered.

Skylar released a sigh of relief. "Okay. I was just wondering," she said and quickly hugged him. "Love you. See you later. Tell Torin I said don't have too much fun."

He chuckled. "A'ight, I will. I love you, too, Sky."

She went off to do her own thing, and Synovi was grateful. He didn't need her to see him get emotional about her question.

"She'll grow out of asking you that. It's just—"

"A trauma response," Synovi finished her sentence. "She needed the reassurance before I left. I get it."

Simone nodded. "Yeah. But I'll have them there on time."

"You're welcome to stay. I mean, we're family."

"You sure? I don't want to make anyone uncomfortable."

"Nah. You good. Everyone knows you, and Torin won't mind."

She considered his words and nodded. "Okay. Well, I'll be there."

"A'ight. I'ma shake. We got date night and some more stuff planned."

"Okay. Y'all have a good time," she said as they walked toward the door.

Before they could get there, Kalie hollered from the couch, "Bye, TorNovi!"

"See you later, KK!" Synovi shouted, then chuckled. "That lil' girl, man."

"Is something special."

"They both are."

Finally, back inside the truck, Synovi headed to Torin's crib so they could get ready for their date night. Even though they'd taken on so much responsibility and ran successful businesses, they still made time to enjoy each other. They were too young and in their bags to always focus on work. It was time to enjoy the fruits of their labor.

As much as she claimed she didn't like the club, Torin was having a blast inside their section at Lavish. They went out to eat before heading to the club, and she was throwing ass like she hadn't eaten almost all of her full-course meal. Leighton was hyping her up by her side as the DJ spun "Throw It! Remix" by Spiffy The Goat and Big Boss Vette.

"I don't need no beat, I'ma hype my bestie up! Throw that ass, friend!" Leighton cheered.

Torin did just that. With a dangerous arch in her back, she bounced her ass to the beat like she was a professional twerker. Synovi didn't miss a beat as he held her waist. He let her show out and smirked when she tossed her bundles to one side and looked over her shoulder at him. He smacked her ass for some encouragement.

Sitting on the couch, Synovi had a perfect view of her pussy print in the tan jumpsuit she was wearing. He was tempted to tell her it was time to go the way she was putting on a show, but he was enjoying watching her turn up. His eyes were low from the blunt he smoked an hour prior, but he peeped everything, including Torin's movements.

Sexily, she slowed it down and rolled her hips when Big Boss Vette's verse started. When the chorus returned, she vibrated her ass for a few seconds more before falling into Synovi's lap.

"Whew. Am I drunk?" She giggled, leaning her head back on his shoulder.

Synovi placed his large hand against her stomach, holding her wobbling frame in place. "If you gotta ask, you might be." He smirked.

"That's okay, 'cause I know you're going to make sure I'm good."

"Always."

Torin smiled with her eyes shut. *In all ways,* she thought.

His hand trailed up her body, discreetly cupping one of her breasts. The action was so normal to him that he and Torin momentarily forgot where they were. She let him feel her up, loving the massage he was giving her boob. Synovi was grateful the club was dimly lit.

"Girl!" Leighton shrieked, grabbing ahold of her hand. "Get up. We didn't come out to be laid up."

Torin gave her a lazy grin. "Shut up. I was catching my breath."

"Well, I hope it's caught because— Oh, this is our shit! Okay, DJ!"

When "Planet Rock" by Tech N9ne came on, the entire club was on their feet grooving. A true KC legend in the music industry, he had the club jumping per usual. Whenever this song came on, young and old people showed out.

Torin caught her second wind and didn't take a seat until the DJ slowed it down ten minutes later. She was now sitting next to Synovi with her legs crossed. Drunkenly, she dug in the pocket of his black pants, searching for nothing in particular. Just doing shit that she knew he wouldn't mind.

"You good, Love?" Synovi asked.

Torin nodded. "Mhm. Thank you for tonight. I had fun. Ooh, and I have my leftovers in the car."

"You can't wait to smash them, huh?" He chuckled.

"Sure can't." She yawned.

"Let me know when you ready to leave and we can slide."

"Okay."

Grabbing her bottle of water off the table, Torin took a generous sip and put the cap back on. Her eyes roamed their section, ready to let Leighton know they were about to head out, when they fell on a gorgeous dark-skinned beauty with the coldest, slim-thick shape. She was staring Torin down like there was a problem, and she hoped like hell there wasn't one because she solved those. Her jet-black thirty-inch bust-down install seemed to blow with each step she took their way.

"I know she's not walking over here," Torin muttered, making Synovi extra alert.

The last party scene he was at with her, Jade's crazy ass, hawked them down in the parking lot. His focus was now on the woman approaching them. A light-skinned man he'd never seen before was at her side when they stepped before them.

"I just had to come over here and tell you that you are fine as hell," the woman said confidently. She spoke loud enough for Torin and Synovi to hear her.

There was a slight slur in her words, and Synovi

figured that had to be why she was so bold, but he didn't know her like that. The liquor had nothing to do with her approach.

"Thank you so much. You are, too," Torin smiled, seductively eyeing her.

"Mamas, come on. We ain't doing this shit tonight," Parish grumbled. "Aye, my fault, cuz," he told Synovi.

"It's all good," Synovi replied coolly.

"Did you used to be a dancer? Because I was watching you bounce that ass on your man and baby, yes, ma'am," Koya hyped.

Torin laughed. "Not at all, but I could've been one. What's your name? You a dancer?"

"Mhm. For my man. I'm Koya."

"Torin," she said, sticking her hand out.

Synovi lowered it.

"Nah. We don't shake hands and agree on shit with other people."

Koya giggled, not knowing what he meant, but found it cute. "Oop. Okay. Well, can she give me a dance? I know you not trying to keep her all to yourself."

"I am."

Synovi's answer was clear-cut. He looked at Parish, who was shaking his head with an arm draped over Koya's shoulder. Noticing his chill demeanor, Synovi quickly realized Koya's behavior was nothing new.

"A'ight, Mamas. You don' had your fun. Tell her bye," Parish asserted.

Koya smiled and slowly ran her hand down Torin's thigh. "See you later, gorgeous."

Friendly as she wanted to be, Torin waved bye. Curiously, she watched them exit the section, wondering what type of shit they were about to get into. Facing Synovi, she licked her lips and pulled the bottom one between her teeth.

"She was pretty," she stated.

Synovi's head bobbed upward, acknowledging her comment.

"You ever think—"

"Nope." He cut her off.

Laughing, Torin fell all over him. "You didn't even let me finish."

"'Cause I know what you were about to say." Synovi faced her. "I don't like sharing. I'ma selfish type of nigga when it comes to everything about you. Pretty woman or not, I still want you all to my mothafuckin' self."

Synovi kissed her lips and stood from the couch. Torin was stuck. When he started talking like that, making her pussy thump and her heart melt... she knew it was time to go before she showed these folks just how nasty she could get. Synovi stuck his hand out, helping her up.

"Okay. I'm ready to go," she said.

Synovi chuckled, humored by her antics. "Yeah, I bet you are. C'mon, so I can give you this dick and remind you who you and that pussy belong to. We not going out no more." He mumbled jokingly but meant every word before that.

Childishly, Torin clapped her hands and smiled hard. He didn't have to tell her twice.

synovi & torin

A long yawn escaped Torin as she adjusted in the passenger seat of Synovi's truck. She had become a true passenger princess when they went anywhere. After their much-needed weekend to themselves, Sunday was finally here, and all Torin wanted to do was lay in bed. They'd been there most of the morning, cuddling and discussing the upcoming week.

It was one of their favorite things to do. They finally got up when Tracee called, telling them to come over for brunch. Torin was all for a home-cooked meal, especially if her mama was preparing it.

"We should've gone to get the girls," she suggested.

"Nah. Let them chill. We can pick them up when we leave here."

Torin fake pouted, acting just like Kalie did when she didn't get her way. When the girls were gone, she missed them and wanted to pick them up as early as possible. They were now a staple in her life, and Torin loved how her family accepted them as their own.

If Synovi ever needed a favor or had questions, he could always call on Tracee or Mr. K. Seeing the people he'd grown to love treat his sisters like family warmed his heart like no other.

"Ooh. I hope she made some fried potatoes," Torin said as they pulled on her mama's block. Seeing all the cars lining the curbs, she got excited and then worried immediately after.

"Why you looking like that?" Synovi asked, parking in the empty spot in the driveway.

"The last time my mama had the family over, she told us some bad news," Torin sighed.

Cutting the engine, Synovi cleared his throat. "Let's not think the worst. She might just want everyone over to spend time."

Torin hoped that was it. Synovi exited the truck and came around to open her door. On the walk to the front door, Torin mumbled incoherent words the entire way. Synovi didn't know what she was nervous about, but he hoped the feeling didn't last or settle. She called out for her mama as soon as she crossed the threshold.

"Mommy!" Torin yelled, going to search for her.

Synovi chuckled behind her and exhaled a deep breath.

"I'm in here!" Tracee yelled back.

Not hearing any other voices, she frowned. Torin was confused as to why it was so quiet when she saw all those cars outside. Stepping inside the living room, her jaw dropped at the same time as the beat to "I'm In Love" by Ginuwine did.

You know, baby. I'm so in love with you.

"Wait," Torin whispered, catching the hints.

Her hand flew to her chest, trying to calm her thundering heart. She hadn't even noticed the rose petals decorating the floor nor the bouquet of tulips in her daddy's hand. Her eyes blurred with wetness, now aware of the many standing faces with their phones out, recording this special moment.

And I want the world to know it, know what I mean?

Torin's hands trembled. She inhaled a stuttered breath, seeing the girls holding signs. Kalie held one that said, "Will You," while Skylar held another that read *Marry Me?*

And there's a lot that I wanna say to you, too. So, listen closely. Okay?

Patting her cheeks, Torin pivoted to face the man in charge of her wet lashes and pounding heart. Synovi greeted her with a confident smile. It was one of a man who knew who he wanted to spend the rest of his life with.

"My Love," Synovi said sweetly, walking to her.

Torin was immobile and inconsolably shedding tears. Wiping her cheeks, he kissed her lips. "Relax."

"You said we were getting brunch." Torin cried, making some folks chuckle. "You tricked me."

"I had to. I told you I was going to change your last name, and I meant that," he said, clearing his throat.

His eyes misted, and Torin quickly consoled him. She rubbed a hand down his neck, and Synovi bent his head, pressing his forehead against hers. No words were spoken; just energy transferred. Getting himself together, Synovi pulled away first and lowered to the ground.

"Okaaay! I know that's right!" Leighton cheered.

"Yeah, my boy. Gon' head and wife sis' up," D'Marco encouraged.

The couple smirked at the encouraging hoots and hollers before they tuned everyone out.

"Remember that day you asked me why I call you Love? I told you it was because that's what you are... that's what you feel like. I mean that. You embody everything it's meant to be and then some."

Torin wanted them to disappear so no one could bear witness to the words he was feeding her soul. She was addicted, and Synovi was her drug of choice in high dosages only. Torin wanted to inject this man into her veins.

"God couldn't have crafted a more perfect, selfless, goofy, hardworking, supportive, determined, patient, and good-hearted woman. I had a lot more words, but you get what I'm saying."

They shared a laugh, easing both of their nervousness.

"You've made me a better man. Inspire me to keep going, and the shit is so natural for you. That makes loving you easy, baby. You're beautiful not only on the outside but on the inside, too. Yo' soul is one of none."

Torin could've passed out. He knew what his words did to her, and Synovi kept going. Expressing himself hadn't been an issue for quite a while now, and today wasn't the day he'd stop.

"I never knew the type of peace and comfort another

human could bring me until I met you. You show up and bring light to my darkest moments, reminding me that there's no love there. We don't even have to speak when I'm with you; your presence fills the void."

"My God," Torin whispered, dripping tears on his arm as he held her hand. She fanned her face and blew out a breath.

"I thank Him every day for you. Twice, 'cause you deserve that. You deserve the world, no lie. As much as you give, you deserve someone who vows to always commit and pour into you. I'ma do that. Whatever you want, whatever you need, I want to provide it until I can't. What I'm trying to say is... Love, will you marry me? You said Mrs. B had a nice ring to it; I'm tryna see."

Digging in his pocket, Synovi pulled out a black velvet box. Flipping the lid, he exposed a stunning two-carat, princess-cut cathedral ring. Torin didn't care about the ring, even though she caught the glint of it trying to outshine her man.

"Yes. Of course, I will," she answered without hesitating.

He couldn't slide the ring on before Torin launched herself into him. She hugged him tightly and gave him the biggest kiss, not believing this moment. Synovi had utterly blindsided her in the best way. He gave the love she gave him back tenfold with no conditions.

It was never a question of whether Torin felt his love because, like her... he too now felt like it. It bounced off him in waves that Torin was no longer afraid she'd drown in.

Applause echoed around them, bringing them back

from the world they escaped to. Torin looked down at her ring and then up at Synovi.

She smirked. "It's so beautiful and elegant."

"I do what I can," he wisecracked.

Now that her eyes were no longer filled with tears, Torin took in the people standing around. Mr. K was there with his wife, looking like the proudest father in the world. It was crazy to witness Synovi's transformation, especially from his point of view, but he loved it. Otherwise, he wouldn't have given him his blessing.

D'Marco, Nikki, Ms. Reid, her husband, and their baby, GiGi, Mia, Eboni, Boss, Racquel, and many others were in attendance. Tracee even had Unique on a video call, watching from prison. She made sure Unique didn't miss this moment. Simone was also there and shook her head when Kalie moved from her side.

She made her way through the crowd and looked up at Torin.

"Hi, KK!"

With squinted eyes, Kalie grabbed Torin's hand. She twisted it, admiring the sparkle and clarity. "It's so pretty. Do I get one, too?"

Synovi chuckled. "Yeah. I'll get you one, too."

"Don't forget about me," Skylar said, making herself known.

"Never that. Thank y'all for holding the signs."

While Torin was sleeping, Simone called once they got to Tracee's and had him explain everything. Synovi wanted to tell them before now, but the girls were unpredictable. He would've been hurt had they spilled the tea on accident.

The couple made eye contact as their family and friends gushed over their proposal and setup. Torin felt like she was floating. They tuned out again, and Synovi kissed her cheek.

"I love you so much," Torin cooed, on the verge of crying again.

"I love you more, Love. Always?"

She smirked and nodded.

"In all ways."

He didn't have to ask. Torin would keep giving him her love until she physically couldn't. Synovi had rightfully earned the privilege.

The end.

To own **physical paperback and hardback copies,** visit my website.

acknowledgments

Thank You!

Thank you to every reader who took a chance on Keep You To Myself! Your unwavering love and support mean so much to me. More than words can express. I'm truly honored and grateful that God placed it on my heart to share Synovi & Torin's story with the world. It's been in the making since last year, and I can finally rest knowing I did the story justice. I'm fulfilled... for now.
If you enjoyed this book, please be sure to leave a rating/review if you can.

To my cover reveal team, thank y'all! If "show out then" was a person, it's ya'll. The pure excitement y'all had gearing up for release day warmed my heart and had me in awe. You ladies are beyond talented with the graphics and visuals. Let me find out I need to hire some of y'all. (Gives side eye)
To my friends & family who held it down... y'all the realest. I love y'all! Always. In all ways.

Special shoutout to GH, Sequaia, Ebony, Ciera, Julia, Miesha, Lydia, Torri, and Victoria. I appreciate you ladies so much!

Interested in some of the characters mentioned in the book? Tap their names below and enjoy their stories.
Projex & Loriana - From The Hood With Love series
Koya & Parish - Trappin' Through The Snow series

stay connected with briann danae

Follow me on Instagram, TikTok & Facebook to stay updated on all things book-related.
Just in case you're not on social media, subscribe to my mailing list so you won't miss a thing.

www.ingramcontent.com/pod-product-compliance
Lightning Source LLC
Chambersburg PA
CBHW032126020826
49184CB00037B/373

* 9 7 9 8 9 9 1 8 0 1 2 5 6 *